Her heart said he wouldn't harm her, but everything else inside her said he was a brutal killer...

Suddenly, awareness tingled across her skin, a touch as warm as flame. She stopped abruptly, looking up. Shadows haunted the entrance of the building, and though there was little to be seen through the rain and the gloom, she knew someone stood there. Not because she could smell him, but because she could *feel* him.

A figure detached itself from the blackness and moved into the light. Her heart did an uneven little dance, and suddenly air seemed a precious commodity.

Grey.

Here.

Waiting for her.

Eryn took a step back, then stopped. From the moment she'd met him, she'd believed deep down that he meant her no harm. She believed that still.

But why was he here, and how did he even know where she lived?

His beautiful face was carefully blank, and the storm-clad eyes were just as neutral. Yet his emotions swam around her, touching her senses as surely as the crisp air chilled her skin. His determination was something she could almost taste, his desire a wall of heat that made her heart sing. Yet it was the slight edge of hesitancy that hit her the hardest.

He wasn't here by choice. Given the choice, he'd rather be anywhere else.

"That's true, but not for the reasons you suspect," he said, his voice a soft, deep growl that made her knees feel weak.

She ignored the sensation, and said flatly, "You're reading my mind." Which was an obvious statement, but right then, she couldn't think of anything to say *but* the obvious.

He nodded. Slivers of sunshine seemed to dance in his rain-darkened hair. "We've formed a connection."

Something in his low voice suggested he wasn't all that happy about it, and she felt invisible hackles rise.

With thanks to my family, my editor, Linda,
and my agent, Miriam.

Other Books
by Keri Arthur

Nikki & Michael Series
Dancing with the Devil
Hearts in Darkness
Chasing the Shadows
Kiss the Night Good-bye

Damask Circle Series
Circle of Fire
Circle of Death
Circle of Desire

Werewolf Series
Beneath a Rising Moon
Beneath a Darkening Moon

Urban Fantasy Series
Memory Zero
Generation 18
Penumbra

LifeMate Connections:
Eryn

***

Keri Arthur

LifeMate Connections: Eryn
Published by ImaJinn Books

10 Digit ISBN: 1-933417-23-4
13 Digit ISBN: 978-1-933417-23-3

10 9 8 7 6 5 4 3 2 1

PUBLISHER'S NOTE:
This book is a work of fiction. Names, characters, places and incidents are products of the author's imagination or are used fictitiously. Any resemblance to actual events or locales or persons, living or dead, is entirely coincidental.

Books are available at quantity discounts when used to promote products or services. For information please write to: Marketing Division, ImaJinn Books, P.O. Box 545, Canon City, CO 81212, or call toll free 1-877-625-3592.

Cover design by Patricia Lazarus

ImaJinn Books
P.O. Box 545, Canon City, CO 81212
Toll Free: 1-877-625-3592
http://www.imajinnbooks.com

One

The wind was blowing a gale and the night was not only bitter, but wet as well. Eryn swiped at the water dripping off her nose and fleetingly wished she hadn't agreed to this assignment. She would much rather be home, curled up in front of a blazing fire, book and coffee in hand, than standing here in the pouring rain, waiting for a go ahead.

She shoved her freezing hands into her pockets and studied the building opposite. It was nothing out of the ordinary—just a plain brown-brick warehouse that had recently been converted into a bar. When originally built, the warehouse had sat on the edge of what had been one of the trendiest areas of town, but now, thanks to falling population numbers, it was well outside city limits.

The old fashioned lantern lights on either side of the bar's red metal doors cast warm shadows across the wet night, and through the semi-fogged windows that lined the front of the old building, people were visible, laughing, dancing, and generally having a good time. She'd be warm enough once she got inside.

If she ever got inside.

She raised a hand, lightly touching the silver stud in her left ear. "I'm freezing my butt off here, Jack. Are the suspects inside or not?"

"One is." The deep voice practically blasted into her right ear. "We're checking for the rest."

She winced and twisted the stud, adjusting the volume. "Which one is in?"

"Gray eyes."

Eryn half smiled. They'd taken to calling him that simply because the man seemed to have at least five names, and none of them actually existed beyond a driver's license and a

passport. There was some suspicion he might be military or
covert operations, but there was little in the way of help or
information currently coming from those two areas.

"Harrison and Gantry nowhere in sight?"

"Not yet."

A droplet of water slid past the collar of her coat and
down her neck. She shivered. "I'm going to look like a
drowned mutt soon if we don't get moving."

"Darlin', even drowned you'd look damn delicious."

"Gee, thanks," she said dryly. "But compliments aren't
going to get you into my pants."

"Can't blame an old man for trying."

Eryn snorted softly. With men now outnumbering women
ten to one—thanks to the stupid one-child-per-family rule
governments the world over had introduced generations ago
in an effort to control population growth—*trying* was a good
word to describe the whole male-female relationship
experience. That rule no longer existed, thank God, but the
damage had been done already. The only good thing about
the out-of-kilter balance was that women could now pick
and choose as they pleased, and female promiscuity was no
longer frowned upon. In fact, it was positively encouraged.
There were even some sectors of the government who were
currently trying to pass a law that women could not settle
down with one particular man unless they'd had at least fifteen
previous partners.

Talk about men being afraid of never getting their end in,
she thought grimly.

This bar, LifeMate Connections, and others like it, were
one of the recent solutions for those men and women who
actually *wanted* to settle down and have a family. The three-
story building was not only a bar, but a hotel, with monitored
bedrooms and security close by. Women could "test drive"
the various offers without having to risk taking strangers home.
And, thanks to the strict medical checks everyone underwent

on joining, they also knew all the men inside were not only free of disease, but extremely fertile, which was important in an age of declining fertility. Once a woman had found a man she thought might make a suitable mate, she could then explore the relationship beyond the secure realms of the bar.

Only that decision had recently ended up getting five women killed.

The task force had been formed as soon as it became clear they had a serial killer on the loose, and had the brief to *"do anything necessary"* to catch the killer. Eryn hadn't been involved in early investigations, which wasn't a surprise since she was a medical secretary at the coroner's office, not an investigator. She was only here now because she was a shifter with a keen sense of smell. The murderer left few clues, and they needed someone with a hound's nose to sort through the scents in the victims' apartments and pick out the ones that didn't seem to belong. It wasn't the first time she'd been asked to do this, and it probably wouldn't be the last. And as long as she wasn't expected to go in when the scent of death was fresh and ripe, she was fine with it. At least it was a change from boring office duties.

But the only aroma she'd been able to pick up in all five apartments was an odd one—a springtime, blossomy sort of smell that seemed more suitable for a female than a male.

Maybe their killer was bisexual, though from all accounts, neither Harrison nor Gantry were.

But the other reason she'd been selected was because she was in her late twenties, with brown-black hair and green eyes. Just the type the killer seemed to prefer.

Of course, despite the "do anything" brief, they couldn't actually force her to become a decoy. Nor could they actually demand that she go into the club and flirt with men who might well be murderers. Especially when everyone knew that flirting might not be all she had to do.

So, they'd outlined their plan and given her the option to "volunteer." Which she had, all too readily. Besides the fact that she trusted her instincts and her nose to keep her out of a murderer's bed, this was a once in a lifetime opportunity to experience what went on in the LifeMate bars without actually having to pay for it. You had to be a member to get into them, and membership was expensive. More than *she* could currently afford, anyway, even with the female discount. Though, like most women, she *was* saving for that moment in the future when she decided to settle down and have a kid.

She shifted her weight from one foot to another, then said, "Are we going or not? I've been standing here for over five minutes. If anyone happens to be watching, that's going to appear more than a little suspicious."

"The go ahead just came through, even though gray eyes is still the only suspect there. Remember to keep the mike open."

"You're just a bunch of dirty old men who want to get their rocks off if I happen to get laid."

And once she'd sniffed out gray eyes, that was certainly the plan. Hell, she'd been celibate for so long she was beginning to think there was something wrong with her. The fact that most of the people she worked with were boring old scientists didn't help. Add to that the long hours she'd been working of late, and you had long term frustration. Hell, these last few days had been the first time in six months she'd come within touching distance of decent looking men—and she couldn't play with them because of the department's rule of no fraternizing. A rule she wasn't about to break, because even if the people she worked with were boring, the job itself paid well, and she wasn't inundated with a whirlwind of different scents everyday. A coroner's office might not be the best place for a shifter with a keen nose to work, but it was a hell of a lot easier to deal with than an office building filled with scent-wearing humans. Now, *that* was hard to cope with.

So, once she'd given gray eyes the metaphorical thumbs up or thumbs down, she was going to see what offers came her way and take a few of them for a test run. The powers that be could hardly complain when that's exactly what they put her in there for. And she could always argue that she was merely ensuring her cover stayed intact.

"Listening and watching other people having sex is the only joy we old men get these days," Jack replied dryly. "Don't you know it's the only reason we arrange these little excursions?"

She grinned as she crossed the road. At thirty-five, Jack could hardly be described as old, though his silvery hair gave him a distinguished appearance—at least until you looked past the hair and saw the sexy twinkle in his blue eyes, and the "come-get-me" smile. "You got a position on gray eyes?"

"He's in a booth at the rear right of the bar."

"Alone?"

"For the moment, yes."

"Has he been alone all night?"

"Been up to the bar a few times, getting drinks and talking to a few of the ladies there, but otherwise, yes."

"You think he's waiting for someone?"

"Who knows? Besides, the bar's security cams cover the upstairs areas more than the bar itself. He might have met someone and we just didn't see it."

"The bar's not fully covered because the action happens upstairs rather than downstairs."

"Not all the time, lassie." Jack's voice was filled with amusement. "Some pretty erotic things happen on the dance floor, and in those back booths."

"Sounds to me like you've already got your rocks off tonight."

"I love my job," he said solemnly.

She snorted and put a hand on the door. "Heading in now. Talk to you later."

She touched the right stud, turning the voice-receive off, then pushed open the heavy red door.

Warmth rushed out, chasing the chill from her face, surrounding her in a honeyed heat that almost instantly made her want to shuck off her coat.

She stepped inside and closed the door. It was then that the many aromas hit and giddiness rushed over her. Mix layer upon layer of perfume and aftershave with the scent of humanity, alcohol and desire, and you had a somewhat lethal combination. At least to a shifter whose sense of smell was as sensitive as hers.

She left her hand on the door, using it as a support as she battled the dizziness. Why hadn't she thought to shield her olfactory sense? God, she knew better than to walk into *any* public area with all senses on high—and shielding was something she'd learned to do when she was still a pup.

Maybe it was the excitement of the chase. Or maybe it was the prospect of finally being able to ease a few basic aches that had made her forget. Either way, it was stupid, because she was here to chase a killer, not just a scent, and she had to remember that at all times. And she should have thought to mention to Jack that shielding meant her sense of smell wouldn't work unless she was *extremely* close to the subject.

Kissing a murderer was not something she really wanted to do, but she'd do that, and more, if that's what it took to stop this sick fiend from killing again. She might not have seen the bodies, but she'd seen the photos, and that was more than enough to wash away any doubts she had about her part in this. At least she had basic cop training—all employees at the coroner's office nowadays did—and she certainly had the strength to protect herself.

And while some in the task force weren't entirely convinced that the smell she'd caught belonged to the killer, she was, if only because that springtime scent had held an undertone of death. And if the suspects didn't match that smell, then hey, she possibly had three very hunky men with which to play.

When the dizziness abated, she unbuttoned her coat and watched a security officer approach.

"First time here?" he said, checking her pass, then taking her coat and offering a ticket in exchange.

"Yes."

"First drink is complimentary, then. Just head on over to the bar and they'll scan your pass and give you whatever you want."

She gave him a dimpled smile and watched the heat flare in his brown eyes. After six months of flying solo, it was nice to know she could still affect the opposite sex so readily. "Thanks."

He nodded and walked into the cloak room. She headed down the steps, but hesitated on the bottom one, allowing her gaze to sweep the room.

A long mahogany bar dominated the right side of the room. Every woman who stood there had a good eight or nine men surrounding her. Half a dozen barpersons tended to these customers, all of them women dressed in barely there outfits. Maybe to give those gentlemen who were missing out something to look at.

Warm light infused the rest of the room, giving everything a golden glow, but leaving shadows haunting the distant corners. Tables clustered the front section near the door and windows, but these gave way to booths that lined the walls, leaving plenty of room for a dance floor.

She couldn't actually see the DJ, though she knew he was here somewhere. The music throbbing across the babble of conversation filled the air with lustful melodies designed to seduce the senses and get bodies swaying. It ran across her skin as sensually as a lover's kiss, making her tingle. Ache, almost.

She closed her eyes, took a careful breath, inhaling the muted, but nevertheless rich aromas of desire and sex. God, it had been *too* long since she'd indulged her sensual side. Shifters, no matter what the breed, tended to have an extremely high sex drive, and for far too long, she'd overlooked hers.

Well, not tonight. Not if she had *anything* to say about it.

She walked across to the bar to collect her drink—choosing French champagne, which was usually way out of her price range—then moved toward the crowd edging the dance floor.

At least half a dozen men immediately gravitated towards her. Knowing she couldn't head directly for gray eyes, she did nothing more than chat, enjoying their attention and their looks. Enjoying the heady smell of masculinity and arousal that swirled around her, making her pulse race. But gradually, she moved on, talking and flirting as she did so, but always heading toward the rear booths and bachelor number one.

Only she didn't have to go that far, because suddenly he was walking through the crowd towards her. She stopped, gaze widening, her heart leaping to the vicinity of her throat and seeming to lodge there. The images she'd seen of him on the com-screens never could have prepared her for the reality—the potency—of the man himself.

He was tall and powerfully built, with chiseled features and dark golden hair. He moved with the lightness of a vampire, yet instinct suggested he was a shifter, just like her. What breed of shifter she couldn't say, and right then, didn't care. Not when the sheer sexual energy radiating off him burned her skin as sharply as a flame.

Their gazes met, and he paused, staring at her, his beautiful face expressionless, yet his storm-clad eyes filling with such desire it curled her toes.

And all she wanted to do was reach for him, touch him, feel the warm strength of his body pressed firmly against hers.

Damn, this was unlike *anything* she'd ever experienced before. Lust at first sight wasn't new—hell, she was a shifter, a mutt, and instant attraction came with the territory. But this was more than that. Not just lust, but something else, something deeper. It was almost as if they were attracted on levels that went far beyond base need.

In some respects, that was scary, if only because the man her hormones had latched onto with such ferocity might well be a killer.

God, fate wouldn't be such a bitch, would it?

He started moving again, and her gaze traveled downwards, admiring the way his burgundy sweater clung to his body, emphasizing the width of his shoulders and his powerful arms. The way his jeans hugged his hips, highlighting not only the lean strength of his legs, but the size of his packaging. Damn, he was well built—in *all* areas.

He stopped when there were still several feet between them, his gaze sliding casually down her body. Heat prickled across her skin, firmly igniting the deep down ache. Her nipples hardened, pressing almost painfully against the sheer material of her dress. The throbbing ache got stronger, especially when his gaze seemed to linger on her hips. For the first time she wondered just how transparent the damp dress was. Wondered if he could see she was wearing nothing underneath.

Then his gaze rose to hers again, and the desire so evident in his stormy eyes echoed right through her. Lust ignited the air between them, caressing her skin with heat until it felt like she was glowing.

He smiled slowly, intimately, and her already erratic pulse tripped into overdrive. It was the sort of smile that might be shared by two lovers after a night of incredible sex, and that was exactly the message his smile was meant to portray. And she sensed it *would* be extraordinary between them. That he would more than live up to the promises made by his heated gaze and sexy smile.

"Grey Stockard." He offered his hand, his voice low and rich, thrumming through her as warmly as a summer breeze.

Grey? Was it merely coincidence that they'd picked his name without even knowing it? *If* that was his real name, of course. "Eryn James."

His fingers were long and strong, and so hot they seemed to wrap hers in an inferno. And suddenly she was fighting images of those fingers sliding across her skin, exploring and caressing and teasing. Oh, how she wanted that. Wanted to be touched by this man.

She swallowed, battling to keep on an even keel, battling to remember why she was here and who he might be.

"Pleasure to meet you," he said, raising her hand to his lips, his breath warm against her knuckles as he brushed the sweetest of kisses across her fingertips.

God, her heart was hammering so hard it felt as if it would jump out of her chest.

"Care to dance?" he continued softly

Only if dancing was a euphemism for let's get down and have wild sex.

She hastily drank some champagne, but it did little to ease the dryness in her throat or the deeper down burning. "I thought you were on your way somewhere else."

"Only for a drink." The smile that tugged his lips was so damn sensuous her knees threatened to give way. "And only because I had nothing better to do."

Oh, she could think of *lots* of things he could do... She swallowed another hasty gulp of champagne, and felt the buzz start in her head. Only she wasn't sure whether it was the alcohol or the closeness of the man.

Somehow, she managed to say, "And you've found something better now?"

"I believe I might have. If she's willing."

The wicked gleam in his eyes told her he wasn't just talking about dancing, and her pulse rate soared even higher.

"She is." *Very* willing. She finished her drink in another large gulp that made her head spin even more.

"Good."

He plucked the glass from her hand, put it on a table in a nearby booth, then led her into the thick of the dance floor, right into the very heart of the crush, until it seemed everyone was pressing and touching everyone else, and the smell of desire was so powerful it was almost liquid. Heat swirled around her, through her, until it was impossible to tell whether the hunger flaming her skin was hers or his or the crowd's.

But however fiercely she wanted him, she was not so far gone that she lost *all* sense of danger. She had to be careful. Had to. Then he wrapped an arm around her waist and pulled her close, and suddenly the need to be careful was all but lost to the smell of raw virility and thick need. She closed her eyes, losing herself in the aroma, allowing it to wash through her pores and set her body alight even more.

Until she realized something was missing.

His *scent*.

Which was ridiculous. *Everyone* had a scent, and it was as individual as a fingerprint. But underneath the sheer male smell, there was nothing. Maybe the heat surrounding her, drowning her, was affecting her senses.

He began to move in time to the music, and she swayed with him. But it wasn't dancing, as such. With the crowd pressed so close, true dancing had become impossible. Besides, the way their bodies brushed was far too intimate, far too erotic, to come under the label of simple dancing.

After a while, he raised a hand and brushed the strands of hair from her cheek. Her skin quivered, burned, where he touched. "Do you come here often?"

I plan to come tonight, and often, she thought, but somehow kept the words inside. "First time. You?"

"Been here for just over a week."

And the murders had started just over two weeks ago. But did that put him in the clear? Especially when he might have been visiting other LifeMate bars? Damn it, had anyone bothered checking that the dead women hadn't visited any other bars? It hadn't been mentioned in the reports she'd read.

"If you've been here that long, I'm surprised you haven't been gobbled up."

His gray eyes gleamed with amusement. "Oh, a few ladies have tried that. And as much as I enjoyed the experience, they weren't what I was looking for."

She had sudden visions of taking the thick hardness of his cock in her mouth, teasing him and tasting him as he teased and tasted her. Sweat prickled across her skin and the deep down ache became positively painful. And while it was against protocol to do that sort of thing here on the dance floor, she was sorely tempted to rush him upstairs and grab a room.

Somehow, she managed to restrain the urge and after thrusting the enticing images from her mind, said, "So, what are you looking for?"

"I'm not really sure I'm actually looking." His hand slid from her back to her butt, branding her skin through the thin fibers of her dress and sending delicious slivers of anticipation thrumming through her.

Then he pulled her tighter against him, so close that she was breathing in as he breathed out, and the wild beat of his heart echoed hers. His body was warm and hard, and the thick heat of his erection rubbed erotically against her belly. God, how she wished they were naked. Wished he was inside, not outside.

She again managed to drag her mind from the sexual mire it was seeping into, and raised an eyebrow. "Then why are you here?"

He shrugged. "I was curious."

He was also lying. Why she was so certain, she couldn't really say. She'd always been intuitive, but this went deeper. It was almost as if she tasted the lie in his words, and that was odd indeed.

But if he hadn't come here to find a mate, what had he come here for? To hunt down his next victim?

She didn't want to believe that—she really didn't. Yet it was a possibility she *had* to consider.

"You're spending a lot of money just to satisfy curiosity."

He shrugged again. "If you've got it, why not use it?"

Why not indeed. And did that mean he was so rich that the price this place charged was little more than petty cash? "If you *were* looking, what would your type be?"

His eyes gleamed with amusement. "Someone who could get me hot enough to come with just a look."

He was teasing, *and* avoiding the question. Obviously, a man who didn't want to be pinned down. So how did he become a member? The bar telepathically screened all applicants to ensure those applying actually wanted kids. That they weren't just using the bar as a free sex service. How did Grey slip through their nets?

"And have you ever found someone like that?"

"Up until now, no."

The heat in his gaze was growing in intensity, sending burning waves of desire lapping across her skin. She licked her lips, saw his gaze drop, felt the hunger sizzling the air leap several more notches. God, she wished she had a drink. Wished she could just throw caution to the wind.

"So you've never actually dated any of the women here?"

His gaze jumped back to hers, the gray depths suddenly holding the chill of winter. "No. Why do you ask?"

"Just curious. A few of the men I talked to earlier said they'd tried it, but it hadn't worked out in the end."

"Really?"

He was suspicious. Not that it showed in his voice or his expression. It was just something she felt.

Why would he be suspicious if he was innocent?

Tension slivered through her. "Yes, really."

He studied her for a second, gaze steely. "You wouldn't happen to be a security officer testing me out, would you?"

She blinked. "What?"

His grip tightened on her rear, becoming almost painful. "You heard. Are you, or are you not, security?"

"Not. And why would security be checking you out?"

"Because it's policy to randomly check new applicants to ensure browsers haven't slipped through the net."

By browsers did he mean those who just wanted an easy lay rather than commitment? And why would he think the club did that? She wasn't aware of it, and she'd been briefed by the manager on not only all the club's rules and regs, but on the clubs layout and security.

"Well, given that you are browsing, I can see why you'd be a little worried by the thought of me being security."

His smile was a slow burn of heat, and some of the tension she'd felt in him eased. But not all. He was still wary, and she again wondered why.

"A security officer is not someone I'd prefer to meet. Not until I find what I'm looking for, anyway."

And he *was* looking, just not for a mate or children, but something else entirely different. Entirely darker.

A chill ran through her. Why was she getting these little intuitive flashes? It was not something she'd been prone to in the past. Not so clearly, anyway.

"I can play a security officer, if you'd like," she said, keeping her voice light. Teasing. "Want me to haul you away and interrogate you?"

His head lowered so that his breath caressed her mouth, and his lips brushed hers as he spoke. "Interrogation was not what I had in mind."

Her mind was shouting *Yes! Yes!* even as she asked, "What did you have in mind, then?"

"This."

His mouth came down on hers. Not gently, not tentatively, but forcefully. He was a man who knew exactly what he wanted, exactly what *she* wanted, and his kiss reflected that. It was urgent, hungry, his mouth plundering hers as their tongues tangled, tasted, teased. And while it was everything she wanted, it also made her want a whole lot more. Made her want him more.

God, the man could kiss.

After what seemed like hours they came up for air. The rapid pounding of her heart was a cadence that seemed to override the babble of voices and the heavy, erotic music that swirled around them. The scent of desire was so thick, so strong, that all she could think about was how much she needed this man to finish what he'd started. Lord, she literally *ached*. She needed to touch, and be touched, and she needed it as badly as she needed air.

It didn't matter that he was a suspect, that he didn't have a scent, that he'd lied to her more than once, and probably wasn't who he said he was. Lust was all consuming, and it was beginning to swamp all common sense.

"I want to fuck you," he said, his breath whispering heat across her lips. "Right here, right now."

His coarse words made desire boil over. Oh God... she *so* wanted the same. But while desire might be all consuming, she knew right here and right now wasn't exactly the right thing to do. "That's against the rules."

"Look around us. Others are doing it."

"Just because others are doing it doesn't make it right. It could get us thrown out." And in truth, that was the *only* thing stopping her. She was here to do a job, and she couldn't do that job if she was banned.

"I thought you were here to get down and have wild sex?"

Her gaze widened a little. She certainly hadn't said *that* out loud—had he read her thoughts? Or merely her body language? And if he *could* catch her thoughts, would that explain his sudden suspicion? Had he realized she was here for more than what she was saying?

"I *am* here for wild sex."

"Then what's stopping you?"

"I can't afford to get thrown out. I don't have the money to reapply somewhere else."

"We won't get thrown out."

"You can't guarantee that."

"Yes, I can."

There was something in his voice that made her want to believe him. Or was that merely her hormones willing her to listen to any lie in their quest for satisfaction? "How can you be so sure? Are you the owner?"

He grinned. "I know the owner. Trust me, she won't throw us out."

The words were barely out of his mouth when he kissed her again, and whatever slivers of control she had were totally and irrevocably smashed by the force of that kiss. By the desire and passion behind it.

"Let's do it," he said into her mouth, the thick heat of his erection grinding so sensually against her belly.

"Yes," she said quickly, knowing if she didn't she might well combust.

She slid her hands to his hips and pulled down his zipper, freeing him from the constraint of his jeans. He lifted her up onto him. And then he was in her, filling her, and it felt so good. So very, very good. She wrapped her legs around his waist, pushing him deeper still, until it felt as if the long length of him was going to spear right through her body. His thick groan of pleasure was a sound she echoed. God, having a man so deep inside was *far* better than she remembered.

And definitely far better than the goddamn vibrators she'd been using as a substitute.

He began to move, thrusting so deliciously deep, and thought slipped away. All she could do was move with him, savoring and enjoying the sensations flowing through her. But slow and sensuous sex was not what she wanted—or needed—right now. Not after six frustrating months of flying solo. She moved against him, taking control of the rhythm, ramping up the speed. Needing it hard, needing it fast. He matched her movements, thrusting quicker, deeper, until her whole body quivered with the force of it, and she was panting, sweating, aching with the need for completion.

God, the heat of him, the feel of so much hard flesh pressed against her, inside and out, felt so good, so incredibly good, that she just didn't want it to stop. But it would stop, because the low down trembling was growing, fanning upwards from the hotspot where their bodies met, a wave of heat that seemed to suck the breath from her lungs. The sheer intensity of the sensations swamping her had her grabbing his shoulders, her fingers digging through his sweater, into his flesh.

"Oh God." Her voice was little more than a fractured whisper. "Make me come. Please make me..."

The rest of her plea was lost to a kiss that was savage, urgent, and as glorious as the sex they were sharing. Their already frantic tempo increased, his penis ramming deep, so gloriously deep inside, reaching places she'd swear had never been touched before now. And then suddenly she couldn't think, couldn't breathe, couldn't do anything except merely feel as her climax came, sending her spiraling into a place that was sheer, unadulterated bliss. A second later he went rigid against her, the force of his release tearing a long, deep groan from his throat.

It was yet another sound she echoed. She rested her forehead against his chest, listening to the wild beat of his heart, knowing her own was just as erratic. And in the ashes of that glorious aftermath, she hoped like hell she hadn't just fucked a murderer.

The stud in her right ear suddenly went hot. Jack, wanting to talk to her. She sighed, and raised her head.

"Well, that scratched an itch."

He kissed her nose, then released her, holding her arm until she'd found her land legs again. "Why don't we take this upstairs and ease a few more?"

The burning in her ear was getting stronger. Jack, getting impatient. She wrinkled her nose and tried for a teasing smile. "It's my first night here, you know. I'd like to try a few offers, rather than settle for the first one."

His smile held a hint of arrogance. "Ah, but when you test the best first, why try anything else?"

She raised an eyebrow. "But how do I know the first offer is the best until I try the others?"

"Try them tomorrow night."

"I'll go to the restroom and think about it."

"I'll book a room."

"No guarantee I'll be there." Though she wanted to be. Oh, how she wanted to be. It just depended on what Jack wanted.

"I'll chance that."

"It's your money." She stepped back, even though it was the last thing she really wanted to do. As sated as she was, part of her knew they'd only just scratched the surface when it came to how good they could be together. "How will I find you if I decide to take up the offer?"

"The security officer will escort you to my room."

She nodded, but as she turned to go, he tugged her back towards him and kissed her. It was an affirmation of intent that left her shaken *and* stirred.

"No promises," she said, and was a little annoyed to hear the breathless edge in her voice. Damn it, she was here to do a job, and however much this man might affect her, she had to remember he was a suspect. She had to be careful around him.

A thought that hadn't exactly worried her a few moments ago. God, what kind of fool was she?

The horny kind, that's what. And after six months in isolation, her hormones were reasserting control with a vengeance. But they might just have targeted the wrong man.

"If you don't find me," he said. "I'll find you."

There was an edge in his voice that sent a tremor across her skin. But it wasn't caused so much by the passion in his voice but, rather, the almost calculating glint in his eyes.

This man was definitely after something more than sex. And if that glint was anything to go by, he suspected that she was here for something more than what she was saying, too.

Maybe fate could be a bitch after all.

Two

Eryn fled to the restroom. After checking to ensure no one was there, she leaned against the vanity and let out a long, slow breath. Where had men like Grey been hiding all her life? Suspect or not, the man wasn't only seriously sexy, but he was seriously dangerous when it came to her blood pressure. And he certainly knew how to show a woman a good time—even in a short amount of time.

Which begged the question—why come here for sex? Surely a man with his prowess and looks only had to crook a finger and he'd have a dozen eager women panting for his every attention—imbalance of the sexes or not.

It just didn't make any sense, especially when he'd admitted he wasn't here to find a partner with whom he could have children.

Frowning lightly, she did a quick clean up, then twisted the right ear stud. "What?"

"Having a good time, are we?" Jack's voice was dry.

"The question is, are you?" she retorted.

"Well, actually, the boys and I thought you could be a bit more vocal. Silent panting just doesn't do the job."

"Tough. I'm not a screamer." Though she had been known to yodel on occasion. It was an unfortunate side effect of being a beagle shifter. "And if you called me away to say that, I'm going to bite you next time I see you."

"I might enjoy it."

"I very much doubt it. Being bitten by a hound dog ain't quite the same as being bitten by a woman."

"I guess not." Amusement touched his voice. "We did a search on his name."

"And?"

"Grey Stockard doesn't exist."

Surprise, surprise. "How many aliases can one man have?"

"A few, apparently."

"But he does use Grey on most of them, so maybe that's his real first name."

"Possibly. But a search on the name Grey revealed thousands and thousands of them. Apparently, it was one of the more popular choices thirty to thirty five years ago."

Which was about the age Grey looked—though with shifters, you never really could be sure, as we tend to age at a far slower rate than humans. "What about his claim of knowing the owner?"

"We're checking that right now."

"What about his claim that security cruise through the bar looking for browsers?"

"The club never mentioned that sort of security arrangement, but then, they may not have figured it important."

"Even the smallest tidbit could be important on a case like this, couldn't it?" Especially if the killer turned out to be one of the browsing security officers.

"Yes. You got anything for us?"

"Yeah, he has no scent." She closed her eyes, imagining herself in his arms again, surrounded by his heat, the raw sensual smell of him that was not his actual scent, but delicious all the same. Desire stirred in her veins, a reminder that she'd only just knocked the edge off need. Complete satisfaction was a long way off yet. And, unfortunately, she very much suspected there was only one man who could fill the demands of her body.

"What do you mean?" Jack asked.

"It's like he's been wiped clean. There's nothing on him." Nothing to track him by, which might well be the point.

"Is something like that usual?"

"No, it's extremely *un*usual."

"Meaning he's done it on purpose?"

"Very likely." Though how on earth did you erase a base

scent?

"Then we track him once he comes out of that bar, and see if we can actually get something on him."

"You'd better use a good tracker. He's a shifter of some kind and may well sense them."

"So we use a bird shifter."

"It'd be a good idea." At least Grey wouldn't scent a bird. "Is that all you buzzed for?"

"No. Harrison just walked into the bar. Go suss him out."

"And leave Grey? Won't that make him suspicious?"

"Can't see why. You made it clear you were here to play the field for a while."

Yeah, but she didn't want to play the field. She only wanted to play with Grey. Which was a big bad when she knew absolutely nothing about the man.

"Give me a position on Harrison."

"Table near the corner window."

"I'll go give him a sniff."

"Do that, and report back. We'll see where we go from there."

She knew where *she* wanted to go from there. To bed. With Grey. "Turning you off again."

"Darlin', you could never turn me off."

She grinned. She'd learned very early on that Jack was a serial flirt. As long as they were female, he didn't seem to care whether they were young, old, beautiful or plain. He treated them all to the same level of sexy banter. Why he was still single she had no idea. The man was definitely a good catch—though, unfortunately, not her type. If she ever did settle down, it would be with another shifter, not a human. She'd seen enough mixed marriages fizzle out to not want to try one herself.

"Jack, you're incorrigible."

"That's the nicest thing anyone has said to me—does that mean we can get down and get dirty?"

She laughed. "No, it does not."

"Damn."

"Bye Jack."

She turned off the receive and checked her reflection in the mirror. The heat in her cheeks had faded a little, but not the excited gleam in her eyes. She looked like a women on the hunt, which she supposed she was. Only the object of her lust was not a man she could see at this particular point in time.

She sighed, ran her fingers through her short hair to settle it back into place, then headed out into the main bar area again, grabbing a drink before moving on in search of her quarry.

Harrison was one of several men clustered around a petite blonde. Eryn flared her nostrils, carefully searching the scents swirling around her, working through the thick maze of flowers, forest, and fruits, finally catching a brief, tantalizing taste of the one she was looking for. But the slither was gone before she could pinpoint a direction. Frowning, she looked around to ensure no one was watching her, then she slopped half of her drink on the floor. She took a step, pretended to slide, and cannoned into Harrison's hard form with a grunt. There wasn't much fat on the man, that was for sure.

"Hey, careful there, little lady," he said, his hands firm on her arms as he caught and righted her.

"Sorry," she said, forcing contriteness into her voice. "I slid on the wet floor."

Keeping one hand on her arm, he frowned down at the floorboards. "Some idiot must have spilt their drink. We'd better get someone to clean that before somebody gets hurt."

His voice was rich, and held a twang that reminded her of the Old West. In his faded denims, blue checked shirt and brown boots, he certainly fit the image of a cowboy. Only she had a suspicion the brown mop of hair had never been restrained by a hat, and that the shiny boots hadn't even tread across a well kept lawn, let alone the wilds of a cattle ranch.

He snapped his fingers, calling over a waitress, then his blue gaze settled on her. As handsome as his rugged features were, there was damn little in the way of response from her hormones. Maybe they were still too busy languishing in the afterglow of her brief time with Grey.

She raised a hand and brushed the droplets of wine from his shirt. His body was taut under the cotton fabric, his muscles well defined. "Lucky it's not red."

His grin was decidedly roughish. "It's only an old shirt anyways." He stuck out a huge hand. "Tate Harrison, at your service."

"Eryn James." She shook his hand, feeling the calluses across his palm. He might not be a cowboy, but he definitely wasn't a paper pusher, either. She lowered her shields a little, trying to catch his scent without getting too close. The air was a riot of aromas. They were too close to the blonde and her entourage for her to pinpoint his scent from everyone else's. "Listen, why don't we go over to the bar, and I'll buy you a drink to apologize for spilling mine all over you."

"Apologies aren't necessary, but I'm more than happy to accompany you to the bar."

He touched a hand to her back and guided her forward. His fingers were pleasantly warm through the gauzy material of her dress, but didn't brand her the way Grey's had.

Damn it, why was her mind so fixated on the man?

They found an untaken space down near the end of the bar, and she ordered herself a wine and him a beer.

He hunkered down a little, his shoulders brushing hers as he leaned muscular forearms on the mahogany surface and wrapped a paw around his drink. "You been coming here long?"

She met his gaze, seeing the blatant interest there and half wishing she could respond more than mildly. The man was first rate in the rugged looks department, and she very much suspected that if she hadn't met Grey first, her hormones might have latched onto a man like this.

But then, given the long drought they'd been suffering, they might have latched onto any man she found even remotely attractive. "First night."

"Ah. So you're merely testing the waters."

She nodded. "And I have no intention of settling on one overture until I test all those on offer."

"That goes without saying." He took a drink of beer, then added, "You looking for anything in particular?"

She couldn't help smiling. "Won't know that until I find it."

"Good. You'd be amazed at how many women come in here with preconceived ideas about what—who—would make a suitable mate."

She raised an eyebrow at the edge in his voice. "You sound more than a little peeved by that."

"Hell, yeah. Preconceived notions cut down the options—for all of us."

"So you haven't had much luck here yourself?"

He shook his head. "Of course, I'm not here all that regular. I've spent time with eight or nine ladies, but nothing has ever eventuated."

"Beyond the realms of the bar, you mean?"

He nodded and raised a large hand. "Seems the hands of a plumber aren't what ladies want these days."

She raised a hand, placing her palm against his. His fingers dwarfed hers. "Then those ladies are idiots. I can't imagine the plumbing trade becoming obsolete any time soon, and you guys are certainly raking it in when it comes to the money side of things."

He grinned. "Most women don't realize that."

"Maybe you'd better start mentioning it."

"I just might." His fingers enclosed around hers. "Is my current company at all interested in plumbers?"

"She would be, if she didn't already have an offer on the

table tonight."

"And he let you walk away from him? The man is a fool."

"Well, he did have to arrange a room."

"Little lady, if you'd agreed to be mine for the night, there'd be no way in hell I'd let you leave my side until I got you into a room and had my wicked way with you."

She had a vision of his rough hands skimming across her naked, burning skin, and her pulse leapt. Maybe she wasn't as immune to this man as she'd thought.

She raised an eyebrow, a grin teasing her lips. "And would it be wicked?"

His blue gaze practically smoldered. "Wicked *and* wild. That's a promise."

She drew his hand close, kissing his fingers, drawing in his scent as she did so. Beneath the rich aroma of man was the delicious hint of musk and earthiness. And no hint of the cloying smell of death.

Not the murderer, then. Which made him safe to play with, if she chose to do so.

"I might just hold you to that promise."

"Please do."

She untwined her fingers from his and picked up her drink. "Will you be here tomorrow night?"

"Probably not. But I might be able to make it Monday."

"Then maybe I'll see you then."

He nodded. "If I'm here, and you're here, you can bet your boots I'll be seeing you."

She grinned and raised her glass. "To the possibility of Monday night, then."

He clinked his glass against hers. "And to the prospect of wild and wicked sex."

Oh, yes, please. But the image that darted through her mind was not that of the man who stood in front of her. She rose on her toes and kissed his suntanned cheek, drawing in his scent again just to be sure. Definitely no springtime, definitely no hint of death, and definitely safe to play with.

But safe wasn't what her hormones wanted, apparently.

Drink in hand, she made her way back to the restroom. This time it was occupied, so she had to wait several minutes before it was secure enough to get in contact with Jack.

"It's not Harrison," she said, when she could.

"You sure?"

"Yes. Death is not a smell you can easily hide, and our murderer was entrenched in it." So entrenched, she suspected it was the evil in his soul she was sensing more than his actual scent.

"Which leaves us with Stockard and Gantry. If either of them aren't the killer, we're in the shit."

"Was this the only bar all five women attended?"

"Afraid so. And the only men all five saw are our three current suspects."

"Grey said he's only been here for a week."

"Grey lied."

"But why lie over something as simple as that?"

"Darlin, if I knew that, I could probably tell you whether he was our murderer or not."

She frowned. Somehow, she suspected the reasons for Grey's lies were a whole lot more complicated than either Jack or she suspected. "Have you been able to confirm whether they saw any of these men outside the bar's limits?"

"Afraid not. He's picking loners, and even though three of the five lived in apartment complexes, none of the neighbors heard or saw anything."

Nothing unusual in that. The head-down-see-nothing attitude seemed to have pervaded society ages ago. "And security cameras?"

"You've read the reports. Most of the complexes were old and didn't have cameras installed in the foyers."

Which was a required feature in all new apartment buildings. Even some of the older buildings were installing them for security purposes—hers had, and she knew many of her neighbors felt safer for it.

"Has Gantry come into the pub yet?"

"No."

"Then what do you want me to do?" Even as she asked the question, part of her was willing him to give the right answer.

"You up to spending more time with Grey?"

She was up, down, and sideways for it. Hell, she was practically combusting at the thought. "You do know I'm a shifter, right?"

She could almost hear the gears in his mind turning, wondering where the hell she was leading with a comment like that. Eventually, he said, voice a little wary, "Yeah. So?"

"So, I haven't had sex in six months."

He burst out laughing. "Damn it, woman, that's an ache I would willingly have eased."

"Intercourse between departmental employees is not currently approved."

"Darlin', for you I'd break the rules."

She grinned. "I thought you loved your job."

"I do. But you're not the only one who's suffering a drought."

"Well, if you stopped listening in on everyone else having sex and started following up some of the offers you get, you wouldn't be suffering a drought."

"But that would mean making an effort. I'm not sure I'm ready for that."

"Then continue to suffer the drought," she said dryly, "because this shifter isn't offering relief."

"Well, damn."

She smiled. "Where's Grey?"

He paused. "Coming out of room three-o-five and heading toward the stairs."

"Looking for me."

"Most likely." Jack hesitated. "You really don't have to

take this any further."

"But if I don't, we may never get any leads on this killer."

"Yeah, but still—"

"Jack, I'm safe in the club, and I'm more than capable of protecting myself outside it. I want this killer stopped as much as the rest of you."

"But bedding suspects goes way beyond the call of duty."

"Not for a shifter," she said dryly. Hell, a shifter in a rutting haze would shag anything with two legs and a dick. Not that she was anywhere near as desperate as that, but given the way her hormones had latched onto Grey, she'd been a lot closer to the mark than she'd thought.

"Shifters have a whole different set of morals when it comes to sex," she continued. Humans might have finally caught on to the "promiscuity is good" attitude, but shifters had been there forever. "That's part of the reason I was picked, wasn't it?"

"Well, that and the fact you resemble the other victims."

"So quit worrying about me, and just start worrying about where you're going to fire those frustrated little sperms of yours when you're listening to me having the best sex of my life."

She cut off the sound of his choked laughter and left the restroom. Grey was making a beeline across the dance floor, heading straight towards her.

How had he known she was in the restroom?

He was still a good ten feet away when the force of him hit her, sucking away her breath and leaving her gasping. Her gaze rose to his. The gray depths smoldered with both desire and annoyance, and his passionate mouth was little more than a thin line. Trouble, with a capital T, headed her way.

And she couldn't wait for it to explode all over her. Or in her, as the case may be.

He stopped so close that all she could smell was heat and lust and man. Her breast brushed against the soft wool of his sweater, sending little tingles of electricity shooting across her body. God, she was puddling with desire for the man, and he hadn't done anything except glare down at her.

What the hell was going on between them? They were complete and utter strangers who'd shared a brief but amazing encounter. Yes, some sort of connection was logical, but this went beyond the usual sexual vibe of shifters. And it was far stronger than anything she'd felt in her life so far.

"I told you I'd come get you if you didn't follow me."

His voice was a low rumble that echoed across the recesses of her mind. It was as if she were somehow feeling his words in her head as well as actually hearing them. She raised an eyebrow, forcing herself to remain still and calm when all she wanted to do was throw herself into this man's arm and beg him to take her.

"And I told you I'd think about it."

"I have a room booked."

"And I have a room full of prospects to explore."

He considered her for a moment, then his gaze slid down her body, taking in every inch, exploring in a way she wished his hands would explore. By the time he'd finished little beads of sweat dotted her body and her breath was little more than pants of desire.

The man was definitely dynamite.

"Tell you what," he said, the smile touching his lips both dangerous and confident. "Give me an hour. If, in that time, I don't manage to give you the best orgasm of your life, you walk free."

Walking right now might be a problem, let alone after she'd spent an hour in his presence. "And if you do manage such a feat, what happens?"

His slow grin became full-blown and damn near blew all her circuitry. "Then you're mine for the entire night."

Oh, yes please...

She took a deep breath, trying to get some air into lungs

that felt as if they were burning. "And how are we going to judge whether you've been successful or not?"

"You're a beagle shifter, aren't you?"

She stared at him for a minute, wondering how he'd known. While shifters innately recognized others of their kind, it was unusual to be able to pinpoint the exact breed. "Yes."

"And beagles yodel when they hit the extremes, don't they?"

Jack was going to have a field day with that bit of news. Especially if she *did* yodel. "Yeah, but we don't want to deafen other patrons." Or turn them off their own activities.

"Our room is shielded against extremes of noise. Shifters attend these bars as often as humans, and the owners do cater for the rutting requirements of different breeds."

Something else the manager hadn't thought to mention when he'd been briefing her. What else had he left out? As she'd said to Jack, even the tiniest bit of info could lead them to the killer.

And she really, *really,* hoped that the killer didn't have wicked gray eyes and a mind-blowing smile.

"Deal?" he asked softly.

"Deal," she said. And hoped like hell she didn't end up regretting it.

He placed a hand on her elbow, his touch seeming to scald her skin as he led her up the stairs and down the long corridor to one of the end rooms. She glanced up, checking the position of the security cams, knowing Jack would be watching through them. She gave him a covert smile and a wink before Grey guided her inside and locked the door behind them.

As rooms went, it was pretty basic. The walls were done in a God-awful red, while the carpet and ceiling were a beige that might once have been white. The bed was king size and covered in plain cotton sheets. There was also a sofa, and to her right, a small bathroom.

"Love the color scheme," she said dryly, raising an eyebrow as she turned to face him. The lust so evident in his expression damn near fried her brains. She swallowed heavily and added, "Was there no other choice?"

"Humans equate red with sexy." He shrugged, his muscles rippling enticingly under his sweater. "And the choice was red, black or white."

"Great color range." Her words came breathless again. He was far too close, and breathing air had become dangerously scant.

"Well, people don't come here to admire the walls."

She certainly hadn't… Thought stuttered to a halt as his hand skimmed her side, then slid up her spine to her dress's zipper.

"And there's only one thing *I* came here to admire," he continued, his voice a low growl that did strange things to her already erratic pulse rate. "Right now, she's far too covered for my liking."

He slid down the zipper with agonizing slowness, then moved his hands back to her shoulders and gently pushed the straps down her arms. The dress shimmied down her body, pooling at her feet. She stepped free and kicked it to one side.

He stood back and his gaze roamed down her once more, taking in her breasts, her curves, her legs, as slowly and as devoutly as a connoisseur of the Old Masters might inspect the Mona Lisa. It was an intimate inspection that made her burn, until she was more than ready to take or be taken. But she had a suspicion that *this* time, hard and fast was not an option.

Unless she forced the issue, which she was more than a little inclined to do. While logically she knew it was impossible for someone to physically explode with lust, that's exactly what she thought might happen if she didn't get some serious loving sooner rather than later.

"Glorious," he whispered, his gaze rising to hers again. "Absolutely glorious."

His words made her heart do strange things. Glorious was not a word she would have used to describe herself, but she certainly loved the way the word sounded on his lips. Loved the way he looked at her as he said it.

Somehow, she found the strength to say, "Equality of the sexes is law rather than an option these days. I demand equal ogling time."

He smiled. "I stripped you, so you should return the favor."

No one *this* sexy had to suggest that twice. She closed the brief distance between them and slid her hands under his sweater. His skin was hot against her palms, his muscles well defined. The sweater bunched against her forearms as she reached his chest, then his shoulders, the wool smelling of masculinity and raw desire. He raised his arms, helping her only when their height difference meant she couldn't tug the sweater free. He tossed it into the corner with her dress as she skimmed her hands back down his chest and washboard abs. Her fingers hit the button on his jeans, the cool metal a sharp contrast against the heat of his skin. Her skin.

She raised her gaze to his as she slowly undid the button and slid down the zipper, watching his pupils expand with desire, until the black had almost covered the storm clad gray.

Hooking her thumbs under the elastic of his shorts, she pushed them and his jeans down his legs with the same sort of agonizing slowness he'd used when he'd been admiring her. Which left her at eye level with his cock. He was thick and hard, and she couldn't wait to get him inside. To feel that hardness probing deep.

But there was some tasting to be done first.

After tossing aside his jeans and shorts, she placed butterfly kisses on both his thighs then ran her tongue across the base of his penis. He jumped, ever so slightly, and his soft groan was both a sound of sheer pleasure and an encouragement to do more.

She smiled and licked her way up and down his shaft, occasionally taking in his balls, enjoying his groans of pleasure, the way his cock leapt, as if straining to reach the warm wetness of her own desire. But she wasn't ready to offer him that yet, simply because he wasn't yet as ready as she to explode. So she laved her tongue back up, and swirled her lips around the tip of him before fully taking him into her mouth.

He thrust in response, his body shaking with the effort of restraint as she rolled her tongue around him, alternately tasting and sucking. His movements were becoming more urgent, the salty taste of him beginning to seep into her mouth, telling her he was close to the edge. But she didn't let him cross it, pulling back instead.

"Tease," he whispered thickly. "Perhaps you need some of your own medicine."

"What I need is you inside, right now."

She wrapped her arms around his neck and clambered up his body, positioning herself above him, then driving him deep. It felt like she was driving hot iron right through the very heart of her. Damn, it was *so* good.

He shuddered, his body responding instinctively, thrusting hard. Then he growled deep and slid his hands to her waist, determinedly pulling her off and placing her back on her feet.

He took a deep breath and released it slowly. It whispered across her cheeks as warmly as sin.

"Hard and fast is not going to make you yodel."

She grasped his cock, sliding her hand up and down, teasing him, caressing him. Wanting him to ache as fiercely as she ached. "Right now, I'll settle for simple satisfaction."

He pulled her hand away. "Damn it, woman, I want the whole night, not an hour. It's yodeling or nothing."

She raised an eyebrow. "You're willing to let me walk out that door right now? Let me find someone else who'll give me what I want?"

"No, I am not." He placed several fingers between her breasts, and gently propelled her backwards. "We had a deal, and you will hold to your side of it."

The backs of her knees hit the side of the bed. He gave her a sexy grin and lightly pushed, so that she fell backwards, then added, "You will yodel before the hour is up."

She arched an eyebrow, a smile teasing her lips. "I don't yodel for just anyone, you know."

"I'm not just anyone." He reached for the bottle of massage oil on the bedside table and flipped the top off. The rich smell of honey and citrus tantalized her senses. "Scoot up the bed and roll over."

She obeyed, her heart tripping so hard it would surely jump out of her chest any minute now. Having this man's hands on her was the closest thing to heaven she could have imagined. Heaven itself would be having him inside, thrusting deep and hard, but he seemed determined to draw this out as long as possible. Which she didn't really mind, despite all her protests.

"But you are just anyone, because I know nothing about you."

He knelt at the end of the bed, poured a large dollop of oil into his hands, and rubbed them together. "There's nothing much to tell."

Somehow, she very much doubted that. This man had as many secrets as his gray eyes had shades. "So you have no existence outside the realm of this club?"

His voice held an odd edge of bitterness. "You could say that. Close your eyes."

She did. He didn't start with her feet, as she'd half expected him to, but her upper legs. His big hands pressing and caressing her thighs, his thumbs scooting along the inside of her leg, teasing her, driving her insane with desire. Her sigh was a thick sound of pleasure and frustration combined.

Yet as much as she'd have loved to simply lay there and enjoy his touch, she couldn't. She was here to question this man, and she had to keep trying to do that, even through the erotic assault on her senses.

"You implied that you're rich. Considering money has never fallen off trees, you must do something to get it."

"My family was wealthy. I inherited it."

The warm scent of honey and citrus curled through the air, arousing her senses almost as much as the steady, teasing closeness of his fingers. But somehow she retained enough presence of mind to continue the conversation. "So your parents are dead?"

He nodded, something she oddly felt rather than saw. "Ages ago."

"In an accident?"

"No, murdered."

His touch lightly skimmed her vagina, teasing her from behind. She shuddered, and somehow resisted the urge to press into his fingers, to shift and make them slide deep inside, to where it ached so very badly. She licked her lips and, voice croaky with desire, said, "Oh. Sorry."

He didn't reply to that, just began working his way up her butt and across her back. Part of her mourned the loss of his touch further down, but his fingers were weaving such a spell that it felt as if she was walking a tightrope above a whirlpool of desire. A rope that was threatening to give way at any moment and plunge her headfirst into those glorious waters.

She wanted to drown in those waters. Just wanted to lay here and enjoy his touch and his presence. Instead, she asked, "Then what do you actually do?"

"Nothing terribly important."

She opened an eye and gave him a mock glare. "I'd really like to know a bit more about the man who intends to make me yodel."

His soft chuckle shivered across her skin and made her heart do strange little turns. "Who I am is not important. What I can do *is*."

"Maybe to you." She paused, then decided to push him a little more. Gentle persuasion certainly wasn't getting her much in the way of information. "You know, I met a rather sexy plumber on the way to the restroom. In two minutes I found out more about him than I have with you in an hour. Maybe I should just leave and seek out a partner more willing to share."

His grip tightened on her shoulder, his touch almost bruising. "You are *mine*."

"*I* belong to *no one* but myself."

The sudden edge of anger in her voice was unforced. If there was one thing guaranteed to raise a shifter's ire, it was the notion of "ownership." Way back in the past, before shifters had gained rights in the eyes of the law, they were considered genetic freaks who were more animal than human, so humans had been able to own, and generally abuse, a shifter as they saw fit. Even now, hundreds of years later, the mere mention of ownership or control was a guarantee of a firefight. And Grey, being a shifter himself, should have known better than to use such a word.

"And if I choose to walk out of here," she continued hotly. "I will do so, and you had better not try to stop me."

He took a deep breath and let it out slowly. His gray eyes showed a moment of indecision, and perhaps just a little frustration, then it was gone, lost to the windy depths.

He raised his hands. "If you want to walk, then do so now." His voice was flat, yet the air between them fairly burned with anger. Not hers. His. And it was aimed as much at himself as her. Odd, to say the least. "Because if you stay," he continued, "you will hold to our bargain. And be very aware of the fact that I intend to make you *mine*."

As much as she tried to retain her anger at his words, she couldn't. How could she, when being his for the night equaled many hours of sensual, erotic delights?

Yet as she continued to stare into the stormy depths of his eyes, she wasn't at all sure he was talking about just a night.

The shiver that ran across her skin was part anticipation, part alarm. And totally stupid. After all, hadn't he already stated he was merely cruising? That he wasn't looking for anything permanent?

For that matter, neither was she. Obviously, common sense had flown out the window in the scramble for satisfaction.

"All I'm asking is a fair exchange of information."

"What I do for a living doesn't affect what we both want—or what I intend to do to you. Why are you so intent on delving into my life, when, right now, all that matters is quenching what lies between us?"

His voice was still flat, but his suspicion wasn't only in his words but swirling in the heated air between them. He was far too wary to be an innocent man, and yet, something within her just couldn't see him as a killer. Not of innocent, lonely women, anyway.

Or did she simply want to believe that so she could be free to enjoy his touch without regret, without worry?

"I don't think wanting to know a little more about you is unreasonable. Even if both of us know nothing will come of this liaison." She sat up. "This is ridiculous. I don't even know why I'm here."

He raised an eyebrow at that, an almost condescending smile touching his luscious lips. "You're here for the same reason I am. Amazing sex."

True, but he was here for reasons other than sex. Exactly what those reasons might be was what *she* had to uncover. Amazing sex might be a pleasant by-product of her investigations, but it couldn't be the total sum. Not with this man. "I'm here to find a man to have kids with. You're merely playing. Truth is, I'm wasting my time with you."

"Great sex is never a waste of time."

She swung her legs off the bed and walked over to grab her dress. His expression was amused, as if he didn't really believe she'd actually walk out the door.

And suddenly she knew that's *exactly* what she had to do. The suspicion that stung the air, as well as the way he reacted to personal questions, suggested he was well aware that she was here to find out more about him. It didn't matter why he suspected her, just that he did. And if she wanted to retrieve the situation, she'd have to walk out. Staying would only confirm his suspicions—and that could be dangerous.

"Great sex is something I can find anywhere. I'm after a whole lot more." There was a ring of truth in her words that surprised even her. "Thanks for reminding me about that."

She grabbed her shoes, then turned her back on him and walked out.

And tried to ignore the frustrated screaming of her hormones.

Three

"Well, this is an unexpected turn of events," Jack said into her ear. "Me and the boys were set for a night of blissful sighs and ear-shattering yodels."

"So was I," Eryn said dryly. She pulled herself onto the vanity and leaned back against the mirror. The glass was cool against her spine, and the water she'd splashed her face with earlier dripped from her chin to her chest. Neither one did anything to ease the overheated condition of her skin. "But he's suspicious, and I really had no other option."

"An innocent man had no reason to be suspicious over anything you said."

"I don't think he's the killer."

"Is that intuition or frustration speaking?"

"Both, if I'm at all honest."

"If there's one thing you've been, it's bluntly honest." Amusement touched Jack's deep voice. "And I have to say, it's shocked some of the boys here."

"They need to stop huddling in that van with you and get out in the real world more."

"I keep telling them that, but I think they're enjoying the voyeurism aspects of our job."

"Well, I guess it's cheaper than renting pornos. Where's Grey?"

"Still in the room."

"He's waiting for me to come back." She said it as a statement rather than a question, simply because she sensed it was true. Though *why* he was so confident she would come back was beyond her. They might share a connection that went deeper than the usual sexual link of shifters, but they were still strangers.

"Looks like it," Jack agreed.

"You uncovered any more facts about him yet?"

"We're checking files for unsolved murder cases."

"He didn't say it was unsolved," she interrupted.

"No, but I'm guessing from his tone it was. And given what he said about money, it'll probably be a high society murder, which at least narrows the search field."

"Anything else?"

"No. The man's identity has been wiped clean."

Just like his scent. It had to be deliberate. "There's been no information or help forthcoming from military, FBI or CIA?"

"'They're looking into it' is the latest response. I'm not holding out hope that they'll be much help."

"So you don't think Grey's one of their men?"

"No. But he's somebody's."

She hoped that "somebody" was on the side of good. Hoped Grey was. She had a feeling he'd be a dangerous man to be on the wrong side of.

"So, what do I do now? Leave?"

"I don't think that's an option, given what you told Grey."

She grinned. "Meaning I have permission to go forth and fornicate?"

"You have official approval to do what you have to do to maintain cover."

"Hot damn."

Jack laughed. "Who said undercover work wasn't fun?"

"Not me." She hesitated. "What about Gantry and Harrison?"

"Gantry's still a no show. Harrison's talking to a pretty brunette." He stopped. "Grey's on the move."

"Where?"

"Heading down the stairs."

Her pulse raced with excitement. "Towards the restroom?"

"No."

Damn, she thought, disappointed.

Jack continued, "He's headed towards the back booths.

Seems to be angling toward Harrison."

"What?" Had Grey known Harrison was the man she'd been talking about? If so, how? And what the hell did he intend to do? Warn Harrison off?

"He's just brushed by Harrison and is moving on to the men's room."

Coincidence? Something within her suspected not. Suspected Grey's brief encounter with Harrison had been intentional. Though she had no idea what it meant.

"And Harrison?"

"Still talking to the brunette." He hesitated. "Hang on, he just headed to the restroom."

"You got camera's or listening devices in there?"

"No."

"That's a bit slack."

"People pissing, farting and shitting is not something we need to hear or see. Especially when those people are men."

"Meaning you have devices in the women's room?"

"Well, no. Not for lack of trying, though."

"You're sick, you know that?"

"I try my damnedest."

She grinned. "You think Grey and Harrison know each other?"

"Until we know more about Grey, we won't know."

"But Harrison is who he says he is?"

"Yep."

"You going to have security check out the men's?"

"Who's the cop here?"

"That a trick question?"

He chuckled softly. "You sure you're happy where you are? I'd love to have you on my team."

"Being cooped up in a van with sex-starved men is not my idea of fun."

"We could make it fun." He paused. "Security's just gone in."

Footsteps approached the restroom door. She turned on the tap and scooped up some water. "I'm about to get visitors," she informed Jack. "I'll let you know when it's safe to talk."

Three women pushed through the door, all noise and energy. Eryn splashed the water over herself, closing her eyes and ignoring the three of them as they visited the toilets, washed their hands, and redid their makeup. They were there for a good ten minutes, laughing and chatting like giddy teenagers, though at least one of them was close to forty.

Eryn blew out a relieved breath when they finally left. "Talk to me, Jack."

"Harrison's just come out of the men's room, and Grey's still in there."

"And the security officer?"

"Reports that Grey was chatting on the phone when he walked in, and Harrison was in one of the stalls. Neither man said anything to the other."

"Did security stay in there until Harrison walked out?"

"No. But Harrison came out a few minutes after the security guy. Looks like it was nothing more than a coincidence."

Somehow, she wasn't buying that. "I might go chat some more with Harrison. Where is he now?"

"Up at the bar, getting a drink."

"And the brunette he was chatting up?"

"On the dance floor with another man."

"Good. I might do some more probing, see if he can remember anything about the five victims."

"Just be careful.'"

"Subtle is my middle name."

"Somehow, I doubt that."

She grinned. "So I'll drag him to bed and question him during sex. It's amazing how often truth comes out when the little head is in control."

"I'm not going to dignify that comment with an answer."

"Coward."

"Totally."

She turned off the receiver again and headed out. Pausing just outside the door, she let her gaze roam across the crowded room as she carefully took in the scents.

And just when she least expected it, she caught a wisp of the one she was looking for.

Her heart leapt, then zoomed into high gear. She raised her nose, sniffing lightly as she followed the faint aroma to the right. It led her to the back booths, then drifted away, lost to the unsubtle aromas of flowery perfumes and sweaty sex.

She frowned, glancing around. Two couples inhabited the closest booths, both of them getting down and dirty. The end booth was inhabited by two dark-haired women chatting animatedly.

Grey had been sitting in the end booth earlier this evening. Coincidence? Maybe not. Yet if he was the killer, why couldn't she smell that smell on him?

She opened her senses a little more, but the aromas lining the air were too thick and too layered, threatening sensory overload again. There was no way on Earth she was going to be able to pick out one faint scent in a room as confined as this, no matter how good her nose.

Still, she walked past each of the booths, acting as if she was searching for someone as she carefully tasted the air. And caught the faintest trace of that scent again. She stopped, frowning. It seemed to be coming from the booth with the two women in it. Maybe one of those two had met the murderer sometime during the night.

If that was the case, she'd have to tell Jack. They needed a watch put on both women.

At least her catching the scent meant they were on the right track. The killer had been here sometime in the last few hours—maybe he was still here, somewhere. Given Gantry's nonappearance, that would surely mean he was off the suspect list, right alongside Harrison. Grey was the only one left of the three suspects that she couldn't definitely say yay or nay to.

And if he wasn't the killer, who was? Was it someone all five women had rejected? Surely the police had considered that possibility—though undoubtedly, it would be nigh on impossible to check every single man the five women had mated with at this place. As Jack had pointed out, the security cameras didn't cover all areas. There were lots of nooks and crannies where some loving could be had without the camera catching on.

Which left her with Grey and Harrison. And given Grey's reluctance to answer questions, the only man she could interrogate was Harrison. Though she may have wiped him off the suspect list, maybe he could tell them something that might give them a clue as to who the real killer was.

A long shot, but longs shots were all they really had at this point.

She turned and found her gaze meeting Harrison's. He was still at the bar, but he was looking over his shoulder, and there was something in his gaze that suggested he knew exactly where to find her no matter where she was.

A chill ran up her spine, though she wasn't exactly sure why.

With him watching her so closely, she could hardly disappear into the restroom and ask Jack to keep an eye on the women. Especially since Harrison may have been watching when she'd walked out of the restroom. She may have wiped him off the suspect list, but that didn't mean she was right.

She walked up to him, sliding her hand around his waist as she stopped beside him. The heat of him hit like a club, almost making her gasp. Lord, it was like walking into a furnace of desire.

And that made her frown. Something was very off kilter. He hadn't effected her so strongly before, so why was he doing so now? Or was it merely the fact that the need for satisfaction was growing in intensity, and her hormones were becoming less fussy about where they got it?

She swallowed, then said, in a voice that was a little too husky for her liking, "Care to by a girl a drink?"

His blue eyes met hers. The blatant interest she'd seen earlier was now a bonfire. His lust lashed her skin, making her pulse skip, and race. This man was primed and ready to go—it was just a matter of deciding if she really wanted to go that far.

Though if the desire stirring between them was anything to go by, her hormones had already decided in the affirmative.

"Darlin, you can have anything you want—just as soon as I manage to catch the attention of one of these lovely ladies."

"Easily fixed." Eryn raised two fingers to her lips and gave a shrill whistle. People jumped and stared, but the whistle succeeded in getting them a barperson.

"That's a real handy trick." The amusement crinkling the corners of his blue eyes sent another rush of desire shooting through her veins. "You'll have to teach me."

"It's easy," she teased. "You just put your lips together and blow."

"Keep talking sexy like that and I'm all yours."

She grinned. "Are cowboys really that easy?"

"When you've been on the range with nothing but a horse between your legs and cattle all around you," he drawled, "most definitely."

She laughed. "And has this particular cowboy ever been near a horse or cattle?"

"Only the mechanical kind in country bars."

"Honesty. I like that."

He slid her glass of wine across to her. Their fingers brushed, and electricity skittered across her skin, reigniting the deep-down ache. Damn, what was going on here? Why was she reacting to this man so strongly, when before her reaction was, at best, lukewarm?

He wrapped a hand around his frosty beer. "How come you're down here again? I thought you'd been grabbed for the night."

She shrugged. "Turns out I made the wrong choice."

He raised an eyebrow. "How's that?"

"He wasn't after what I'm after."

"And you know this because...?"

She forced a smile. "Because he let me go."

"A fool indeed." He gave her a look that held enough heat to smoke her insides. "Be assured I will not make the same mistake."

She raised an eyebrow. "Presuming the offer comes to the table."

He hesitated. "Of course."

"And the offer very much depends on how you feel about questions."

"Darlin', with the prospect of wild sex in the offering, you can ask me any damn thing you like."

She leaned a hip against the bar, taking a sip of wine before saying, "You said you've spent time with eight or nine women so far—what went wrong?"

He shrugged. "Everything."

His voice was a little vague, and she frowned. "In what way?"

He hesitated, eyes a little distant, as if he was fighting to find the memories. "Four of them were bi. They weren't looking for anything long term, just a sperm donor."

"Then why did they come here? There're sperm banks all over the place."

"Maybe they wanted a particular look, and that can't be guaranteed at sperm banks." He shrugged again. "Let's not dwell on the past. Let's talk about the future." He half turned, facing her. "Or at least the next few hours."

She raised an eyebrow. "Presuming again that I have a few hours to spare."

"Even the busiest person can make a little time for wild and wicked sex, can't they?"

"Maybe." She sipped her drink, but it did little to ease the aching dryness in her throat. Oh, how she wanted to give in to the desire throbbing through her veins. But as much as her hormones might protest, she was here to do a job. Right now, that job was questioning this man, not shagging him.

"What about the other five tryouts?"

He glanced at his drink, but not before she'd caught the irritated flash in his eyes. "I told you before. The hands of a plumber weren't what they were after."

"There has to be more to it than that."

He looked at her again, but the blue of his eyes was once again distant and, just for a moment, reminded her oddly of Grey. "Why? Women have all the power these days when it comes to relationships, and believe me, they're using it."

She raised an eyebrow. "And you don't like the change? You'd prefer that men once again did all the running in relationships?"

"I believe in equality—in *all* areas."

"Including the bedroom?" She'd met lots of men over the years who'd spouted similar beliefs, but most seemed to get a little ticked off when a woman tried to take control and set the pace. Promiscuity might be required, and women might be able to pick and choose as they pleased, but most men still liked to call the shots when it came to sex.

His brief glance was filled with enough heat to singe her toes. "Particularly in the bedroom."

"Meaning if we went upstairs now, you'd let me take control and do whatever I want to you?"

His gaze met and held hers, and suddenly she couldn't breathe, couldn't think. Could only stare deep into his eyes, until they seemed to surround her, fill her. The world was nothing more than a bluish-gray sea that pounded her skin, and her mind was aflame with the heated wash of his desire.

"Only if you let me do whatever I want to you in return." His words were so softly spoken they seemed nothing more than a lush wind that whispered through her mind.

First it was Grey blowing her sockets, now it was Harrison. Maybe she'd been a whole lot closer to the "shag anything" edge than she'd thought. She blew out a breath, and scrambled to hang onto the last remaining scraps of resistance. "Did you date any of the last five women outside of the bar?"

He reached out, running a finger down her cheek. His eyes were distant, distracted, his touch a sear of lightning against her skin. "No."

"Why not? Did they find someone better?"

"Yes."

Her gaze was still caught in his, and it was getting harder and harder to reach for questions through the lust fogging her brain. She forced a teasing grin and said, "Perhaps you'd better tell me their names, just so I can understand why those women passed up such a fine option."

He grinned. "I'd be a fool if I did."

She raised an eyebrow. "Scared of the competition, cowboy?"

"Right now? No."

His finger had reached her lips and was outlining them. She licked her lips, licked his finger. His skin was cool against her tongue, and tasted faintly of beer and salt. "Then prove it."

His finger paused, his touch branding her lips. "Why is this even important?"

"Because I prefer men not afraid of a challenge." She wrapped her lips around his finger, sucking on it lightly.

The scent of lust sharpened dramatically, drowning her in its heat. "Their names were Gantry and Steepan."

The air around them trembled, as if the flames beginning to consume the two of them were sucking in all available oxygen. It was certainly harder to breathe. To think.

But she had to think. Had to, because he'd just given them something. "And are they here tonight?"

"Gantry's not."

"And Steepan?"

He blinked, and awareness returned to his eyes. He continued to stare at her for a moment, and she'd swear she saw both surprise and anger in his eyes. But once again, that anger wasn't aimed at her, but at himself.

She frowned at the thought. It had been Grey who'd been angry earlier, not Harrison.

"I don't know if Steepan is here or not." He turned away, and picked up his drink.

His lie vibrated through her. He not only knew whether or not Steepan was here, but he actually *knew* him. Not as a friend, but as a...She hesitated, searching for the right word. A colleague. A partner.

And she also knew he wasn't about to tell her more right here and now. Whatever it was that had allowed the slip was now securely locked away.

"Then what *do* you know?"

The sexy smile that suddenly tugged his lips made her heart do a strange little dance. But it wasn't the smile itself, but rather its odd similarity to Grey's smile.

"I know I want to fuck you something fierce."

His words vibrated through her, making the already fierce ache fiercer. "Even with me in full control?"

"Yes."

"Then let's do it." The words were out before she could stop them. But she couldn't regret them, not when the fever of wanting burned through every part of her. Besides, as she'd said to Jack earlier—the best time to question a man was during the haze of sex.

If she could remember the questions.

Something close to triumph blazed in his eyes, then he grabbed her hand, his fingers long, strong and hot as they pressed firmly against hers. He tugged her towards the stairs, not saying a word and not letting her go as he led her up to the second floor, and arranged a room.

Once they were inside the white bedroom, she pulled her hand from his and said, "Strip."

He didn't argue, just silently undressed and tossed his clothes onto the sofa. Then he crossed his arms, watching her as intently as she watched him. A smile tugged her lips. She had a feeling he was ready to stand there all night if that's what it took to convince her he believed in equality in the bedroom. Only equality wasn't the true issue here—it was whether he was willing to allow her to take *complete* control.

She finally allowed her gaze to slide past his face, discovering what she'd instinctively known—that he worthy of a long inspection. Broad shoulders, great arms, powerful chest, slim hips and long, strong legs. And most importantly, impressive packaging. Not the biggest she'd ever seen, but still damn fine. And certainly on a par with Grey.

Her gaze rose to his again. Amusement touched the blue depths, as if he was in on some joke he wasn't about to share.

"Lay down on the bed," she said.

He turned on his heels and walked across the room. She admired his butt as she followed him, then began opening the drawers beside the bed as he lay down. In the second one down, she found what she was looking for—silken rope.

His gaze flickered to the rope and back again. "Remember, what you do to me, I get to do to you."

And didn't *that* thought make her pulse zoom. "The object of this exercise is to discover whether or not you spoke truthfully. Raise your arms above your head."

He did, crossing them at the wrists. "And how is tying my hands going to achieve that?"

She grinned as she roped his hands to the headboards. "It will test your willingness to let a woman be in as complete control as most men like to be."

"I'm not most men."

Grey had basically said the same thing. Was it a phrase they taught in some secret man school or what?

"We shall see." She grabbed two more ropes and tied his feet spread-eagled to the end bedposts. Then she met his gaze across the long hard length of his body.

"Ready?"

A smile tugged one corner of his sensual lips. "I think you can see that I am."

She could. And he was indeed ready—thick, and hard, and pulsing with heat. Suddenly thankful she wasn't wearing any panties, she climbed onto the bed and straddled him, pressing herself against the heat of him, sliding him back and forth through her slickness. He began to move with her, and she stopped.

"Don't," she said softly, "move. Just stay still. This one is for me, and me alone."

He didn't say anything, just watched her, an intentness in his gaze that sent a delicious thrill down her spine. She continued to hold his gaze and began to slide up and down his shaft again, watching his pupils dilate with desire and lust, until the blue was almost gone and all that was left was black ringed by silver. Which was odd when his eyes were blue.

But she really wasn't worried by oddities right now, but rather how damn fine everything was feeling. She closed her eyes, concentrating on sensation, concentrating on sliding him back and forth, teasingly touching all the right places, but never for long enough. Pleasure spiraled, and her breath caught, then quickened. She hadn't intended to fly solo all the way, but right now, she just couldn't stop. It felt too good. *He* felt too good, just sliding back and forth, back and forth. A shudder ran through her, and she rubbed against him harder as the sweet pressure began to build low in her stomach and flutter upwards.

"Look at me," he demanded, voice harsh, raw.

She opened her eyes. His gaze consumed her, burned her. The scent of his need swam around her, flaying her skin, flaying her senses, until all she could feel, all she could smell, was his desire. His body quivered beneath her, as if demanding she unleash him, take him. She didn't, losing herself instead to the rapture and power of denying him pleasure, denying them both that moment of complete oneness while at the same time satisfying her own needs. And even though his frustration lashed at her, there was also something fierce in his eyes, as if what she was doing was exactly what he wanted her to do. And that, somehow, he was deriving almost as much pleasure by watching her take what she needed as he would have if he were inside her.

The thought became lost as the waves of pleasure rose and rose, until they were a molten force that would not be denied.

Yet even as her orgasm ripped through her, some small part of her half-wished it was Grey she rode, that it was Grey whom she would soon allow to pleasure her anyway he damn well pleased.

Trust her to be landed with hormones that could never be happy with what they had.

When the trembling eased, she took a deep breath and let it out slowly. Sweat glimmered across the warm gold of his skin, and his body trembled beneath her. His gaze was fierce, hungry. Demanding. A tremor that was all anticipation ran through her. What was still to come would be good. Real good.

"Satisfied?" His voice was a growl that rumbled right through her.

She allowed a small smile to touch her lips. "If you mean am I satisfied that you're willing to let a woman take complete control in the bedroom, then yes, most definitely.

"Good." He tugged on the rope, freeing his hands. "Your turn."

Another tremor of excitement ran through her. The edge in his voice, the heat in his eyes, suggested that her turn would be a long, drawn out seduction, despite the fact that he was quivering with need.

And women had turned away from this man? What kind of fools were they?

She silently offered him her hands. He looped the silken rope around her wrists, then undid the rope around his ankles and shifted so she could lie down.

"On your stomach," he said, voice still rough.

She obeyed, and he straddled her, the heat of him brushing her skin as he leaned forward and loosely looped the rope around the middle post of the headboard.

Then he said, his words little more than a whisper of warmth past her ear, "You will beg me to give you what you denied me."

"I don't beg for anyone," she replied, knowing even as she said it that in her present state, begging was high on the agenda if she didn't get what her body demanded.

"We'll see." His voice held a confidence that made her quiver deep inside. And that quiver had absolutely nothing to do with fear.

She closed her eyes, waiting for his touch. A top popped, and the warm aroma of citrus and sunshine stung the air. She cracked open an eye. What were the odds of two men wanting to do the exact same thing to her?

Then his oiled hands slid over her back, and the question was rolled away by pleasure. She closed her eyes again, all but purring as his fingers worked magic up her back and across her shoulders. By the time he'd finished she wanted him badly, and she couldn't help groaning in frustration when he climbed off.

"And what was wrong with finishing as we were?"

"The fact that you're not ready to beg me for it yet." He slapped her butt lightly. Even the sting of his hand on her flesh had excitement flushing through her body. "Turn around."

She did. He moved down to her feet, tying them spread-eagled, then started the whole massaging process all over again. It was a sensual and erotic experience that had her panting with need and aching like crazy. But still she wasn't ready to beg, and the dangerous glint in his eyes suggested he had no intention of moving on until she did. Part of her *did* want to give him that, to just beg so she could feel the thick heat of him inside. She needed that, needed him thrusting deep, so very, very deep…and yet, there was also something undeniably exquisite in the torture of waiting. In letting the moment, the tension, and the desire build, until there was nothing between them but urgency and need. She might not be far from that point, but she hadn't reached it yet. And obviously, neither had he.

He reached across her and placed the oil back on the bedside table. "Beg for me," he said softly, his words warm whispers across her lips.

"No," she whispered back, then kissed him.

There was nothing soft, nothing sweet, about this kiss, and yet it was incredibly passionate. It was the kiss of lovers, not two strangers making love.

And then he was inside, driving deep, and she was arching up to meet him, wanting everything he could give, as hard and as fast as he could give it.

Only he didn't give her anything else, just pulled out of her, leaving her empty and aching. His teeth nipped her bottom lip lightly when she opened her mouth to protest. "Beg for me," he whispered again.

"No," she panted, squirming beneath him, trying to recapture his cock and drive him home again.

Only she didn't need to. The words were barely out of her mouth when he was ramming hard inside her again. This time, he stroked several times before withdrawing. The man obviously had amazing control.

"Give me what I want," he said, his gaze holding hers, fiercely determined.

"No," she said, wondering why she felt it was so important that she kept resisting. Damn it, she wanted to be fucked hard, he wanted to oblige, and all she had to do was open her mouth and say please.

But something deep inside had decided resistance was important.

He shifted, moving to one side, then slid his hand down her body and into her slickness. She shuddered, enjoying his caress, the press of fingers against her heated, aching flesh. Enjoying the feel of them sliding in and out, in and out, as his thumb flicked teasingly across her clit. Teasing her, making her ache, making her tremble and moan. And stopping each and every time she came close to orgasm.

He didn't ask her again, but in the end, she had no choice but to give him what he wanted. Not when her body was screaming for completion.

"Please," she panted, "I need you...*want you*...inside."

He slid over the top of her, his grin wicked. Victorious. "Are you begging me, Eryn?"

"Yes." God, yes. "Just do it."

With one swift, hard stroke, he was inside, and it felt so good she could only groan. Then he began to move, thrusting deep and strong, and it was fierce, and passionate, and so damn good she wanted to scream.

And though she could barely even breathe let alone scream, she knew *this* was what had been missing in her love life up to now—a sense of connection that almost seemed spiritual. She could *feel* him, not just inside her body, but on the outskirts of her thoughts. As if the linking of flesh had somehow linked their minds. Emotions swirled between them—a kaleidoscope of color that was passion and warmth, even caring, though she couldn't say how that was possible when they didn't even know each other.

Yet she knew she only had to open up and that kaleidoscope would completely fill her, mind, body and soul, making them one in a way mere sex never could.

She didn't reach out. Didn't dare.

Thought slithered away as the pressure began to build. It spiraled upwards, rapidly gaining momentum, until she couldn't breathe, couldn't think, could only wait for the inevitable peak. A peak she leapt over with abandon, twisting and shaking and moaning. He came with her, his roar echoing in her ears as his body slammed into hers and his release flooded so very deep.

When the tremors finally eased, he laughed softly and rested his forehead against hers. "Well, I'm damn glad you finally gave in."

She grinned. "Yeah, so am I."

He dropped a kiss on her forehead and drew back a little. "No yodeling though, which is somewhat disappointing."

She frowned. She'd said that to Grey, not Harrison, so why would he make a comment like that? Or was it simply a matter of him somehow realizing she was a beagle shifter? "I'm not the type of girl who yodels for just anyone, you know."

"I'm not just anyone," he said, a touch of male arrogance in his tone. "Perhaps we need a replay."

She shifted her hips, moving against him. Despite the fact that they'd only just finished making love, he was still quite firm inside her. It wouldn't take much to get him going—just as it wouldn't take much to get her going.

"If the replay is slower, I'm all for it."

He gave her a wicked grin. "If slow is what the lady wants, slow is what the lady gets." He reared back, undid the ties around her legs, then reached forward, undoing the knots around her hands. Then he drew her up onto her knees, and wrapped his arms around her waist. His eyes were more gray than blue, and held an intentness that made her soul shiver. "This time I intend to make you yodel so loud the whole bar will know your pleasure."

Her pulse zoomed at the thought, and she grinned as she wrapped her arms loosely around his neck. "You can try."

He certainly did try.

And he damn well succeeded.

* * * *

Movement woke Eryn many hours later. She cracked open an eye, watching him pad across the room and gather his clothes.

"Where are you going?" she asked softly, a little surprised he'd leave before their time in the room was up.

He barely even glanced at her as he pulled on his jeans. "Work."

She looked at the clock on the bedside table, and frowned. "It's three in the morning and still dark outside."

He hesitated. "Yeah, but there's stuff I have to do before I actually go to work."

He was lying. And the mere fact that she sensed this made her frown. Damn it, Harrison was human, not shifter, and they shouldn't have that sort of connection. If he *was* a shifter, then okay, maybe, as it was a well known fact that shifter pairings often connected on many different levels. But she'd never heard of a human-shifter pairing sharing anything more than great sex.

And while humans were more than capable of psychic abilities, it wasn't telepathy or empathy happening between them. It was something stranger—something deeper.

She sat up, drawing her knees to her chest and hugging them. "What are you working on at the moment?"

He hesitated, and once again that odd, distant look crept into his eyes. "Reinstalling pipes in Tennamar."

Tennamar was one of the old estates built on the fringes of the city, and a good hour's drive away. So, it was logical he'd leave early, considering he had to go home and get all his gear—so why didn't she believe *that* was the reason he was leaving? Why did she believe his reasons for going were a whole lot darker—and more deadly?

"Will you be here tomorrow night?"

Something flashed in his eyes. Regret. Exasperation. Neither of which made any sense. "Yes."

Yet he'd said earlier tonight he wouldn't be back until Monday. That had been the truth. This wasn't. "Then maybe I'll see you here."

"Yes." He strode across the room and leaned down to kiss her. It wasn't the good-bye kiss she'd been expecting, but rather a promise of things to come. He raised a hand, his fingers lightly brushing her cheek, his gaze intent, as if memorizing every curve, every flaw, in her face. "Till next we meet."

He spun before she could speak and walked to the door, his movements grace itself.

She blinked, for the first time realizing what she was seeing.

It wasn't the walk of a plumber with a hankering to be a cowboy.

It was the walk of a man who moved with the grace of a vampire and the power of a shifter.

Grey, not Harrison.

Four

Eryn blinked again, wondering if her imagination was playing tricks.

It wasn't.

That was definitely Grey's walk. And, suddenly, all the other little niggles came flooding back. The ever-changing color of his eyes. The way her hormones had latched onto him after meeting him at the bar the second time. The sudden lack of any scent besides masculinity. The deep connection between them.

She wasn't crazy.

It *was* Grey.

He was shifter all right—just not the type she'd presumed. He was a far rarer kind—a face shifter. A man who could assume the identity of any man he touched.

That's why he'd brushed past Harrison. He'd wanted to assume his identity. Which meant Harrison was probably still in the men's room.

She waited until Grey had left the room, then scrambled out of bed to grab her clothes. The footsteps leading away from the room told her Grey was out of earshot.

"Jack, you awake?"

"Like I have any other choice with all the noise you've been making."

"Get security into the men's right now. Before Harrison gets there."

She heard the snap of fingers, then the scramble of movement in the background as Jack said, "Why?"

She grabbed her dress and pulled it on, then hunted around for her shoes. "Because the man I've been with the last few hours wasn't Harrison, but Grey. I'm betting the real Harrison is still in the restroom."

"I think all that sex has blown your circuits."

She grabbed her shoes, dangling them from her fingers as she made her way towards the door. "You ever heard of face shifters?"

"No."

"They're an extremely rare form of shifter who can assume the shape of anyone they touch."

"So why call them face shifters?"

"Because it's their face and hair that changes the most. Generally, the body just shifts its mass around a little, but doesn't actually change shape." Which explained the amusement in the fake Harrison's eyes when he'd first stripped. She should have recognized his body—or, at the very least, his penis and balls, because she'd certainly spent enough time licking her way around both.

Still, who'd have expected Grey to be a face shifter? And that he'd usurp Harrison's position in her bed?

Damn it, why do that? Why bother?

"You think he took Harrison's place to check you out?" Jack asked.

She stopped at the door and peered around. Grey was nowhere in sight. "I really don't know what's going on. You checking out that name he gave us?"

"Steepan? Sure am. So far, it's proving to be another dead end frighteningly similar to Grey."

She padded barefoot down the carpeted hall. "Meaning they might just work together?"

"Could be." Jack hesitated. "Security's just contacted us. Seems you were right. The real Harrison is half undressed, hog-tied and unconscious in one of the stalls."

"Where's Grey then?" She stopped at the top of the stairs, but the right-angle bends prevented her from seeing the entire bar.

"Just did an about face and is heading for the front door."

Meaning he must have seen security going in and guessed

his cover might be blown. "You going to arrest him?"

"If we arrest him for mugging Harrison, we may never get to the bottom of this murder case."

So Jack—or at least the department—still thought Grey was the probable killer. "Have you got someone ready to follow him?"

"The eye is in the air as we speak. Come back to the van, Eryn."

She bit her lip, wanting to follow Grey, yet knowing it wasn't her job. And even though her alternate form was made for hunting, she had to have a scent to follow. Grey was nothing more than a tantalizing hint of masculinity—nice, but difficult to follow on a clear night, let alone a rain soaked one.

"Okay," she said. "Be there in five."

She slipped on her shoes and headed down the stairs. Her gaze automatically went to the door, and at that moment, Grey, still wearing Harrison's form, looked over his shoulder. Even across the distance of the pub, his gaze had the power to rock her. He half raised a hand, as if in good-bye, then seemed to regret the gesture. He cut the movement off abruptly and walked out into the night.

She blew out a breath she hadn't realized she'd been holding, then made her way across the room to collect her coat.

The rain hadn't eased, nor had the wind. Holding the flyaway ends of her coat together, she splashed her way towards the van, cursing and shivering as the fat drops of water slithered past the collar and down her neck.

The van door was flung open as she approached, spilling warm light into the gloom. She stepped into the van and squeezed past Henry's rotund figure, hitting the warm, crowded interior with a sigh of relief.

She shucked off the dripping coat, hanging it on a hook near the door, then squeezed past Bob, Jack's other assistant. He didn't even look at her, his gaze glued to the bank of com-screens in front of him, watching the man who walked with a predator's ease.

"What's he doing?" she asked, plunking onto a chair and scooting it towards Jack.

He glanced at her, a sexy smile touching his lips. "He's walking far too well for a man who's just had several hours of amazing sex."

She raised an eyebrow. "If several hours are all it takes to make you legless, you seriously have to get out of this van and start working on your sexual fitness."

"Ain't that a fact." He glanced back at the com-screen. "He's heading down seventh."

"No detours? No car?"

"Not so far."

She raised her gaze to the image on the screen. "He knows he's being watched."

Jack frowned. "How? We're using a hawk shifter. In this weather, he shouldn't be able to see him, let alone scent him."

"Grey's not that kind a shifter."

"Then how could he know he's being followed?"

"I don't know." She raised a hand, tapping the screen with a finger. "But if he didn't know, why hasn't he changed back to his true form?"

"Maybe he can't. Don't some shifters have time restrictions?"

"Only because the sheer mass of their alternate shapes can overtax their hearts. Elephants, for instance."

Jack raised a silvery eyebrow. "Never seen an elephant shifter."

"They're rare."

"As rare as face shifters?"

"No."

Jack crossed his arms and leaned back in the chair. "Seems to me a face shifter might be right at home in the CIA or military."

She nodded. "Even as a cop, they'd be useful. Undercover work would certainly be a whole lot safer if you could just disappear into another identity."

His expression became thoughtful. "You know, we hadn't actually thought to check the files of other departments."

"You think he could be a cop?"

Jack shrugged. "You've been with the man, not me. What does your gut instinct tell you about him?"

She hesitated. She'd worked with cops for nearly nine years now, and Grey just didn't fit the profile. Then again, neither did Jack. But look past the twinkle in Jack's eyes, and you saw the calculation, the distance, that came with being a cop for any length of time. Beyond the occasion flare of lust, Grey's eyes very rarely showed anything. And when they did, it was something altogether darker and more dangerous. He was a killer, but was he a killer of innocents? Somehow, she suspected not.

"If I had to take a guess, I'd say he was a trained operative of some kind."

"Which leads us right back to the military or CIA."

"Or FBI. They have several new paranormal units, don't they?"

"Yeah, but even the new Preternatural Units have to announce their presence to local law enforcement."

"What if Grey is here unofficially?"

He raised an eyebrow. "You think he's here to hunt down the killer?"

"Yes."

Jack studied her for a moment. "Then why bed all the victims?"

"How should I know? Maybe he was feeling horny."

Jack snorted. "Somehow, I think you're making excuses for a man you're rather attracted to."

"Could be." She glanced up at the com-screen. Grey had disappeared. "Where'd he go?"

"Not sure." He leaned the chair back, looking past her. "Bob?"

"Went into the supermarket."

"Is there only one exit?"

"Yep. Though there's an employees exit around the back."

"There any way to keep an eye on that?"

"Henry's checking the traffic and security cameras around the area now."

"Henry, hurry."

"I am, boss, believe me."

Eryn kept her eye on the screen, watching the people come and go. Grey wasn't among them—or was he? As a face shifter, he could assume the shape of any male he touched. He could be the smart-looking black dude moseying out the store right now with his hands filled with grocery bags. Or he could be the gray-haired old man trying to hide the bottle of whisky from his quick-stepping wife.

Her gaze went to the shabby-looking man currently walking though the doors. He carried several bottles of beer, and his thin lips were pursed, as if whistling. Like the others, the body shape was about right, though he looked nothing like Grey. Didn't even walk like him.

Yet she knew, without a doubt, that it was him. How, she couldn't really explain, except to say that something deep inside twitched in recognition.

"There he is," she said, pointing at the fast disappearing figure. "You'd better get someone into the store and check the men's room. I bet he's knocked someone out and taken their clothes."

Jack didn't waste any time refuting her certainty. "Henry, get the cameras on him. Bob, contact our eye and advise him of Grey's change of appearance. And get someone to check the store out." Jack glanced at her. "You want to stick around in case we lose him again?"

She nodded. Going home while it was pouring rain held

no appeal. She didn't have a car and would have to hike several blocks to the subway. And while Jack would undoubtedly arrange a car for her, home didn't have the appeal of sitting here and watching Grey.

Leaning back in her chair, she kicked off her shoes and rested her feet on the corner of the table. "I bet you twenty bucks he'll attempt another changeover in the next ten minutes."

Jack handed her a full coffee mug that had seen better days. "No bet. Henry, make sure you don't lose him."

"We won't."

But after ten minutes of watching, they did. Only Grey didn't go into another store and change form. He simply cut through a tree-filled park, moving beyond the range of the security cameras and their eye in the sky for all of one minute. But one minute was all it took.

Jack swore, and threw down his ear mike in disgust. "There goes our only chance to discover where he lived."

"He'll be back tomorrow night."

Jack glanced at her. "If he knew he was being followed, he might just cut his losses and run."

"He's not your killer. And he'll be back."

"You seem awfully certain of that."

"I am. He's after the killer, same as we are." Only she suspected Grey had no intention of arresting the killer and seeing him brought to trial. No, Grey had something far more permanent in mind.

She sipped her coffee and tried to ignore the chill running down her spine. It was a chill that had nothing to do with the fact that she was lusting after a man who was, by training, a killer, but rather the fact that she kept getting these strange little insights and certainties about a man she only knew sexually.

"So," she added, lifting her feet off the table, "we here again tonight?"

Jack nodded. "Approval's been given. Hopefully Gantry

will make an appearance tonight."

"It's not Gantry."

"And you know this because...?"

"I smelled that smell in the club tonight. It couldn't have been Gantry because he wasn't there."

He gave her a long look. "And you were intending to mention this when?"

"When I remembered it, which I just did." She shrugged an apology. "Trouble is, it was coming from a booth two women were sitting in."

"Which could mean one of those two women has already met the killer."

Especially since both women looked like the type the killer went after. "Might be worth putting a trace on them."

"Which booth were they in?"

"The same one Grey was sitting in earlier. Both women had dark hair. One was in green, the other red."

Jack grunted as he wrote down the information. "We'll grab their pics from the security cams. You want a ride home?"

She hesitated, listening. The rain no longer pounded the van's roof, though the vehicle still trembled under the assault of the wind. She shook her head. "No, I like walking through predawn hours like this. Everything smells so fresh, so new."

"Only a shifter would say something inane like that. The rest of us would be happy to catch a lift so we could get home to the warmth of our beds."

She would have been happy to catch a lift, too, if there'd been someone home to warm her bed. But after too many nights of going to bed alone, and too many mornings of waking alone, she had to catch her pleasures where she could. And there *was* something delicious about walking through the wet hours just before dawn, especially when the rest of the city had yet to stir.

She finished her coffee and placed the cup on the table. "Same bat time?"

Jack nodded and held out a hand. "Ear pieces."

She undid them both and dropped them into his palm. "You and the boys planning to stick around here?"

He glanced at his watch, then nodded. "Changeover is at six."

"Do you really think watching the bar's security cams day and night is going to magically catch the killer?"

He shrugged. "Right now, we've got nothing else. Not unless your nose picks up something, anyway."

"Even a hound has to have a scent to follow. And my nose certainly didn't prove much of a help tonight."

"If you caught the scent once, you'll catch it again. Give it time, Eryn."

Time was the one thing they didn't have much of, because the countdown had begun. The killer was killing a woman every four days. The four-day deadline was up tomorrow...today, she silently amended. But everyone in the van was more than aware of that fact.

"See you tonight."

He nodded and turned back to the screen. She grabbed her coat, pulling it on as she opened the door and stepped into the crisp morning. She took a moment to breathe deep, enjoying the sensation of air so fresh that it was filled with nothing more than the sharp aroma of the passing storm and the warm tang of wet concrete. It wouldn't stay that way for long—even now, the city was stirring. Soon the fumes of cars and factories and life would belch into the air, and this brief moment of revival would be lost for another day.

God, how sad was her life that reveling in a wet dawn was getting to be a high point?

She smiled wryly and shoved her hands into her pockets. Truth was, until this assignment, she hadn't exactly realized how stale her life had become. Yeah, she loved her job, and hell, she loved sunrises, but there was more to life than that. And it was about time she started exploring other avenues of enjoyment.

Like Grey.

She bit her lip and stepped out from the van's cover. The wind blew her hair in a hundred different directions, and her ears, which were oversensitive at the best of times, became chilled. She reached back, snagging the jacket's hood, tugging it over her head and tightening the draw strings.

What good did it do her lusting after Grey? While she couldn't guess at his reasons for bedding the victims, she was positive about one thing. He was here for one reason only— to hunt down a killer. A relationship of *any* kind was not on his agenda.

Which was a damn shame, because the connection that had formed between them in such a brief amount of time suggested even a casual relationship could be a mind-blowing experience.

Still, she at least had the promise of tonight to look forward to.

She splashed across the road, leapt the pool of water gathering around the drain, then continued on towards the subway. Another good thing about traveling at this hour was the lack of people on the trains. Though few people didn't necessarily equate to no aromas. She screwed up her nose, trying to ignore the stale scent of sweat and humanity and old perfume as she traveled the three stops to the station closest to her apartment.

By the time she'd made it out of the subway, it had begun to rain again. A car drove past, splashing a huge wave of water across the pavement, drenching her legs and making her toes even colder than they already were. Strappy high heels and winter weather were *not* a good combination. Note to self, she thought. Tonight bring warm pants and comfy boots to change back into.

She hurried down the street. People were beginning to crowd the pavement, all of them seeming to be in as much a hurry as her to get out of the weather. Her apartment block loomed through a silvery curtain of rain—a dour, ten-story brick building that had absolutely nothing going for it except for the size of the apartments. This close to the city center, space was still a premium and large apartments were rare and costly. But she paid the price willingly, simply because the apartment was not only close to work but at least three parks. Even when space had been at a premium and land prices high, those who had run the city previously had kept the precious parks intact. The outer suburban areas had not fared so well, and there were now few places a shifter could run unless they were willing to drive miles into the countryside. And the cost of gas made that a rare event.

She crossed the street and headed for the building's front steps.

Suddenly, awareness tingled across her skin, a touch as warm as flame. She stopped abruptly, looking up. Shadows haunted the entrance of the building, and though there was little to be seen through the rain and the gloom, she knew someone stood there. Not because she could smell him, but because she could *feel* him.

A figure detached itself from the blackness and moved into the light. Her heart did an uneven little dance, and suddenly air seemed a precious commodity.

Grey.

Here.

Waiting for her.

Eryn took a step back, then stopped. From the moment she'd met him, she'd believed deep down that he meant her no harm. She believed that still.

But why was he here, and how did he even know where she lived?

His beautiful face was carefully blank, and the storm clad eyes were just as neutral. Yet his emotions swam around her, touching her senses as surely as the crisp air chilled her skin.

His determination was something she could almost taste; his desire a wall of heat that made her heart sing. Yet it was the slight edge of hesitancy that hit her the hardest.

He wasn't here by choice. Given the choice, he'd rather be anywhere else.

"That's true, but not for the reasons you suspect," he said, his voice a soft, deep growl that made her knees feel weak.

She ignored the sensation, and said flatly, "You're reading my mind." Which was an obvious statement, but right then, she couldn't think of anything to say *but* the obvious.

He nodded. Slivers of sunshine seemed to dance in his rain-darkened hair. "We've formed a connection."

Something in his low voice suggested he wasn't all that happy about it, and she felt invisible hackles rise. "Some connection—you may know my thoughts, but I sure as hell don't know yours."

"That's because you're not trained to do so."

She raised an eyebrow. "And you are?"

He hesitated, then nodded again. "Look, we need to talk."

"I agree, but there's no way in hell I'm taking you up to my apartment." She wasn't *that* much of a fool.

Annoyance flashed through his eyes. "You're hardly dressed to keep standing here in the rain and cold."

She shrugged and crossed her arms. "I have an alternate shape that doesn't mind this sort of weather."

"I'm not standing here talking to a beagle." He looked to the right. "There's a small diner open just up the road. Why don't we go there for breakfast?"

"Fine." The owner of the diner was a fierce looking ex-boxer whom she knew rather well, since she went there for breakfast most mornings. If she needed help, he'd be there. She stepped back and waved Grey forward. "After you."

Annoyance flashed through his eyes again. He paused briefly, as if he wanted to say something, then moved down the steps. She waited until he was several feet in front of her, then followed. She might be fast, and she might be strong, thanks to her shifter heritage, but he was a big man and moved in a way that suggested speed as well grace. If his intentions were dark, at least the slight distance between them gave her enough of a head start to turn and run.

"You know I mean you no harm." His voice was still flat, yet the air seemed to vibrate with his anger. He didn't like her distrust, and given distrust was totally natural at this point, she had to wonder why.

"No sensible person would trust a man who refuses to answer simple questions."

He glanced over his shoulder. "Yet you had no problem with having sex with me."

She shrugged. "That was in a safe environment."

"Where you were being monitored by the club and your police cohorts."

So he knew. No surprise, really, if he could read her thoughts. "If you know that much, you know precisely why I was there."

"Yeah, I do, and that's what I want to talk to you about."

"Really?" She couldn't help the sliver of disappointment, and perhaps it showed in her voice, because he flashed her a dangerous smile that made her knees go all wobbly again.

"You're a fool if you think that's all I want to discuss with you." He hesitated, his gaze sweeping her, leaving her hot and tingly. "And you do not look like a fool."

"Thanks. I think."

He gave her another pulse-racing smile, then pushed open the diner's door. She followed him inside, and wasn't surprised when he chose a booth in the dimmest corner, as far away from the counter and the few windows as possible. After sliding in opposite him, she tucked her legs underneath the seat. She had a suspicion that if she so much as brushed her legs with his, things might get more than a little heated. And while Dan, the owner, certainly wouldn't mind a free floor show, she didn't want to go down that road until she'd discovered why Grey was really here.

Dan followed them over and handed Grey a tattered menu as he glanced at her. "The usual?"

She nodded. Grey ordered bacon, eggs, and toast, then handed the menu back. She waited until Dan had left, then said, "So, tell me, do you have a real name?"

He hesitated. "Grey."

She raised an eyebrow. "No last name?"

"None that matters anymore."

Or at least, not one that he was willing to trust her with. *That* annoyed her, though given they were only bed buddies, it shouldn't have. If not for the connection between them, it probably wouldn't have.

"Who do you work for?"

Again he hesitated. "I can't tell you that."

"Then what the hell can you tell me?"

He crossed his arms on the table and leaned forward. The heat of him washed over her, along with the wet, raw scent of masculinity. Her pulse skipped and raced harder.

"The person you seek will never be found by you or the police."

She raised an eyebrow at the certainty in his voice. "Because he is too well trained, or because he's a face shifter like you?"

A smile touched his luscious lips. Suddenly, it was all she could do not to lean across the table and claim his mouth with her own.

As if sensing this, desire flared deeper in his eyes until the stormy gray was almost lost to the black. "When did you realize what I was?"

"When I was catching some butt action as you walked out the bedroom door. It wasn't Harrison's walk."

Amusement creased the corners of his eyes, somehow making his almost too perfect features more human. Yet more unforgettable. "Very observant of you. And careless of me."

"Hey, the boys were impressed you could even walk."

His smile grew, and her heart did a strange flutter. This man was dangerous, all right, and not just to her health.

"Which is why I could not retrieve my sweater," he said, his gaze drifting from her face to her breasts and back again.

Suddenly too warm, she peeled off her coat and dropped it on the seat next to her. "How did you lose the cops in the park?"

"How did they find me after the supermarket?"

"I saw you."

He studied her for a moment. "It would seem you are not as oblivious to this link between us as you would have me believe."

That much was certainly true, but she wasn't about to admit it. Giving this man the knowledge of how deeply he affected her would be a bad move on *so* many levels. Not the least of which was the fact that he was a stranger who refused to impart information about himself.

But would that stop her from having sex with him again? Hell, *no!*

"And how did you come to that conclusion?"

"You sensed who I was, didn't you, even though I gave no clues via appearance or walk?"

"Maybe."

A smile tugged his lips again. "I can understand your hesitancy. Believe me, this was not on my agenda, either."

"Then what is?"

His smile faded into something cold and hard. "Catching a killer."

The sudden change was a chilling reminder that she knew nothing about this man other than the fact that he gave good sex. She didn't even know if she could trust him, despite what her instincts said.

She crossed her arms, and leaned back. "Are you

government?"

He paused, his expression assessing. After a moment, he said, "Yes."

"U.S. government, I mean."

"Yes."

"CIA?"

"No."

"FBI?"

"No."

"Who then?"

"It doesn't matter."

It *did* matter, if only because of what was happening between them. She *needed* to know more about him. Needed to explore the possibilities that lay before them.

But that required two willing participants, and she had a suspicion willing wasn't in his repertoire at the moment. So why was he here? Really?

"Do you know the killer?"

"Yes."

"He works with you?"

He hesitated, his gaze sliding past her for a moment, then coming back full of warning. Not that she really needed one when the sound of footsteps, as well as the tantalizing aroma of bacon, pancakes and coffee, was evidence enough that Dan was approaching.

She waited until he'd deposited the food and the coffee, then picked up the small pot of maple syrup and poured it all over her pancakes.

"If you eat a stack like that every morning, piled high with butter and maple syrup, how the hell do you remain so slim?" Grey asked, amusement glinting briefly in his eyes.

"Luck of the draw when it comes to the gene pool. Beagles are naturally slender." She picked up her knife and fork. "You were saying?"

He began to tuck into his bacon and eggs. "You need to

keep away from the bar tonight."

She blinked. "That's not what you were saying."

"No. But it's what I needed to say."

"Why?"

"Because the killer will strike tonight, and I don't want you in the firing line."

His words made her heart do an odd little jig. "Better me than someone who can't defend themselves."

"There is no defense against the likes of this person. Not for you, anyway."

"I'm a shifter. I'm fast. Strong."

His smile held a condescending edge. "Not against this person. Not even against me."

She raised an eyebrow. "You're just a face shifter—no disrespect intended. Granted, you're a male, and therefore stronger than me by nature, but I still should have the edge when it comes to speed."

"You think?"

"I wouldn't have said it otherwise."

He studied her for a moment, his gaze so intent she had to quell the urge to squirm. Then, with a half smile, he put down his knife and fork.

"Care to test that?"

She hesitated. "How?"

"On the count of three, you try to pull your right hand away from the pancakes before I can grab it."

She put down her cutlery. It seemed too easy, which made her suspect it would be the opposite. "Who counts."

He shrugged. "It doesn't matter."

"Okay. One."

He raised an eyebrow, amusement touching his lips again. He crossed his arms, and rested them lightly on the table. It was a pose that suggested this was no contest.

"Two."

Tension ran through her. He still looked relaxed.

LifeMate Connections: Eryn 81

Unconcerned. Like he had all the time in the world to lunge across the table and grab her hand.

"*Three.*"

As fast as she could, she ripped her hand back, out of the way. His hand blurred as it shot out. She got as far as the edge of the table before his fingers wrapped around hers and stopped her dead.

"Damn, that's fast," she muttered, trying to ignore the press of his callused palm against her knuckles. Yet it was impossible to ignore the warm response that spread from her hand to the rest of her body.

"It almost wasn't fast enough." He shifted his grip and, with his thumb, began to lightly caress the inside of her wrist. Her pulse jumped into high gear again, and her throat felt suddenly dry.

"What do you mean?" It came out little more than a husky whisper, and the heat in his gaze went up several notches. Even the air seemed to vibrate with the lust flaring between them.

"You got your hand to the edge of the table. Most people wouldn't have."

"Most people aren't shifters."

"Most shifters aren't that fast." His gaze rose to hers. "Or this beautiful."

For several seconds she lost herself in the ethereal beauty of his eyes, drinking in the heat, the sincerity, the desire, that were all too evident in those ghostly depths.

It would be all too easy to fall for this man.

This stranger.

She blinked and tried to free her hand from his. He held it fast, then with his free hand, pushed the food aside and leaned across the table. She watched his approach, her gaze skating between his lips and his eyes, torn between watching the desire so evident in his gaze, and the advance of the luscious mouth she just wanted to kiss forever. She closed her eyes at the last moment, welcoming his kiss, opening her mouth, drawing him deeper. God, he tasted good. She kissed him long and hard, exploring his mouth with her tongue, tasting him as thoroughly as he tasted her.

By the time he pulled back, her breathing was ragged and tiny beads of perspiration dotted her overheated skin.

"I want you," he whispered, his breath so warm and fast against her lips. He raised a hand, cupping her cheek, his fingers seeming to burn where they touch. "Now."

Oh God...she *so* wanted the same. Yet she couldn't. Not here, not when she knew so little about him. Not when she didn't even know what he really wanted.

He began to drop feather light kisses on her lips, her nose, her cheeks. "Trust your instincts," he said. "They rarely lie."

"It's the rarely bit I'm worried about."

"I'm not lying, Eryn. I want you."

His mouth moved down her neck. She closed her eyes again, enjoying the sensation, feeling warmth flooding all the right places. "That I don't doubt. It's the rest of your story I'm worried about."

"I've told you no lies here."

His tongue skimmed the moisture around the base of her neck. A tremor ran through her. "It's the truths you haven't told that concern me."

"The only truth that matters right now is what's happening between us."

His breath was a warm caress of air against her neck. She licked her lips, fighting the urge to leap across the table and take what he was offering.

"Tell me your name."

He pulled back a little, his gaze searching hers. "It matters that much?"

"Yes."

An oddly pleased smile momentarily tugged his lips. "Grey Harrison James McConnell—the third—at your service."

A laugh bubbled through her. "That's some moniker. No wonder you're reluctant to announce it."

"It's the first time I've told anyone in what seems like ages." He touched her face again, his fingers gentle as he traced a line from her cheek to her lips. "In all honesty, I shouldn't have even told you."

"Then why did you?"

"Because a drowning man should never forsake a life buoy." His words were little more than a whisper against her lips as his mouth claimed hers again. This time, the kiss was a long and sensuous exploration that made her ache for far more than sex. Because this time his kiss held more than just passion.

This time, for the first time, she sensed that he was a kindred spirit in loneliness.

Or was she reading far more into the kiss, and his actions, than she ever should?

Forget doubt. Make love to me, Eryn.

The words were a sensual plea that invaded every corner of her mind. One that made her feel all weak and gooey. She pulled back and took a shuddery breath. Fought to gather the shattered wisps of control.

But where this man was concerned there was no control.

And certainly no backing away from the forest fire they'd started last night.

"On one condition," she somehow managed to say.

"What condition?"

"You answer some questions."

He outlined her lips with a gentle finger, his gaze distracted. "You may not like the answers."

"That doesn't matter. I just need answers."

His finger paused, his gaze suddenly sharpening. "And if I don't give them?"

"Then I walk out the door right now, and you and I are finished."

"That's akin to sexual blackmail."

"No, that's honesty. I may want you, Grey, but I want answers more."

He released a breath that was full of frustration, then sat back and picked up his knife and fork. "Okay. But I could get into deep trouble for it."

She raised an eyebrow. "Then why agree to answer?"

He half smiled. "I'd rather be in trouble with my superiors than have you walk out that door."

His words warmed her in a way his touch hadn't. "How would they even know you've talked to me?"

"They know you've been assigned the case. They will know I've bedded you. It's not hard to put two and two together—unless, of course, you intend to keep what I tell you to yourself."

"You know I can't."

He nodded. "Then it's yet another black blot on my record."

"Sounds like you've got more than one."

"Trouble and I are familiar friends."

"So, who do you work for?"

"That I can't tell you. Not yet. Not until they give clearance."

"So you're some sort of spy? Part of a secret government service?"

"Spy? No. That's CIA territory."

She stared at him, remembering her earlier feelings, remembering her certainty that he was here to find, and kill, their killer.

"You're a hitman. A government hitman."

He grimaced. "Enforcer is a nicer term, but yeah, that's basically what I am."

Her eyes widened at his confirmation. "The government has its own hitmen?"

"There are many evils in this world that the court and the justice system are incapable of dealing with. Evils that the penitentiary system would never be able to hold."

"That doesn't give the government the right to be judge, jury and executioner."

"Would you rather evil be allowed to roam free, creating havoc as it wishes?"

"That depends on what you term evil. And who decides."

"There are rules and checks in place."

She snorted softly. "Like rules ever stopped a government from taking advantage of the system or doing the wrong thing."

"No system is ever one hundred percent accurate. Even the court system." He paused for a moment, eating some of his meal. "Look, I'd rather not get into this any deeper right now. What questions about the case do you have?"

She wolfed down some of her pancakes, barely tasting them, then asked, "If you know for certain the killer will strike tonight, do you also have an inkling of who the victim is?"

He considered her for a moment, expression flat. "Yes."

"How?"

"Our clairvoyants saw their images. There are seven altogether."

"So even though you know the victims, history can't be changed?"

"History can, but it always takes time. Five have died, but there is always the hope we can save the other two."

"Why not tell me so I can tell the police the identities of the other two?"

"Because I'm taking care of it."

She raised an eyebrow. "No, you're not. You're here with—"

She cut off her words, and stared at him.

He smiled grimly. "Yes," he said softly. "You're one of the remaining two slated to die."

Five

Coldness settled in the pit of Eryn's stomach and refused to budge. She put down her knife and fork and pushed the plate to one side. If she ate anything else right now, her stomach might rebel.

"That doesn't make sense. And it certainly doesn't follow the set pattern."

He raised his eyebrows. "You really think there's a pattern in this madness?"

She frowned. "Yeah. The killer has been bedding his victims before he kills them. The only person I was with last night was you."

"Remember what you're dealing with."

She mulled over his statement. "He's assuming the identity of the women's chosen partners?"

"Once they've decided on a mate, yes."

"But why?"

"Because the killer cannot stand them having what..." He paused, as if choosing his words carefully. "...he cannot."

"Children?"

He shook his head. "Love. Acceptance."

Her eyebrows rose. "Acceptance?"

"In a department filled with freaks, your killer is considered the freakiest."

"Why?"

Again, he hesitated. "Because he is something no one thought could exist."

"And that is?"

"Something I can't tell you."

"Can't, or won't?" she snapped.

"Can't." He reached out, capturing her hand before she

could pull it away. His fingers twined around hers, so warm and strong and so, so right. Which was surely a sign her §§§§common sense had flown out the window when it came to this man.

"I have told you more than I should," he said softly. "Any more, and it could be dangerous."

She snorted. "You've just told me I'm slated to die. What could be worse than that?."

"Trust me, there are things far worse than death." He squeezed her fingers. "I come from an organization that has no wish to become known to the general public."

The ice in her stomach grew heavier. "Well, that's a great choice, isn't it? Be killed by our killer, or be killed by the people you work for."

"The people I work for don't kill innocents. But your memories of this time—of us—are certainly under threat."

Her gaze widened in disbelief. "They'd erase it?"

"Definitely." He gave her a lopsided smile that sent her hormones off in an excited little shuffle. "I don't want that. I want you to remember our time together. Want you to remember us."

"Why?"

"Because we're good together."

That they were. But could they be anything more? Somehow, given what he'd said about the department he worked for, she suspected not.

A fierce twinge of regret ran through her. She ignored it and changed tactics. "Why did you bed all the victims?"

"Because my telepathy skills are not strong, and I can generally only read a woman's mind when we are in the midst of making love."

That was an answer she certainly hadn't expected. Though it did explain how he'd known where she lived. "But why did you need to read their minds if you knew who the victims were going to be?"

"What we didn't know was who they'd been with. Or who their chosen partner might be." He shrugged. "It was the fastest way to uncover which men we had to watch."

"Then whoever had the watch assignment wasn't much good, because the women got killed anyway." She frowned. "Were your people actually watching the victims' apartments?"

"Yes."

"Then how did the killer get through?"

"He's a face shifter, and even we can't track all the forms our people are able to take."

She stared at him for a moment. "That's why you don't want the police to catch the killer. Your organization has no intention of letting the authorities suspect that people like you are out there. Or that the people you work for are out there."

He raised her hand to his lips and kissed her fingers. "A quick mind as well as a stunning body. I chose well."

She grinned. "Compliments won't get you said body. But more answers just might."

His eyes gleamed with the hunger that still burned the air between them. "How many more questions must I endure?"

"Six?"

He shook his head, amusement touching the corners of his eyes. "I think I'll need to ease my hunger before I can answer *that* many questions."

"Five, then."

Again he shook his head.

"Four?"

He didn't answer, just gently straightened one of her fingers and raised it to his mouth. His gaze holding hers, he placed her finger in his mouth and lightly sucked on it.

A tremor ran through her. Sweet Lord, this man could get her hot enough to melt without even trying.

She licked her lips. "And you were accusing *me* of sexual blackmail."

He simply gave her a smile that had enough heat to burn

the soles of her feet, and continued doing erotic things to her finger.

"Three?" she somehow managed to croak.

He raised an eyebrow, then released her finger and straightened her hand, placing a gentle kiss on her palm. Desire curled through her, a furnace threatening to explode.

"Two?"

"One," he said, dropping a kiss on the inside of her wrist. "Then we make love."

"Here?"

"The place isn't important."

"It is if it can get us arrested."

"Do you really think the owner will call the police?"

No. He'd sit back and enjoy the show. And give them free coffee as a thank you afterwards. "Why the urgency?"

He gave her another of his mind-blowing smiles. "Because I want you so fiercely it's becoming positively painful."

A feeling she could more than understand. "You'll answer my other questions afterward?"

"If you make love to me again after I answer those questions."

She raised her eyebrows. "Are you always this insatiable?"

"Until I met you, no."

There was no lie in his words, and her heart did another odd dance. "Really?"

"Truly." He released her hand and slid out of the bench seat. Her gaze scooted down his body and she saw that he hadn't been exaggerating. His cock was so hard, his jeans so taught against it, that she could see every little bump in his skin. And oh, how she wanted to feel those bumps inside.

"I've never felt anything like this before," he continued. "I need you as deeply as I need air."

She scooted along the seat as he sat down beside her. "If that's a line, it's a damn good one."

He caught her hand again and tugged her towards him.

She shifted, pressing her back against the table as she straddled him. Or rather, straddled his thick shaft. He kissed her nose, and wrapped his arms around her waist. "No line, just a truth I never expected."

His hands began sliding up her back towards the zipper, and it was becoming hard to think again. "Why?"

"Is that your question?"

His fingers skimmed her skin as he slid the zipper down, sending delicious tremors skating through her body. "No."

He raised his hands to her shoulders, slipping his fingers under the thin straps of her dress then sliding them down her arms. "Then ask it, because I intend to make love to you, and I will not be answering questions during the process."

The dress slithered to her waist, and the air felt gloriously cool against her suddenly bared skin. She arched her back, thrusting her breasts toward him. The heat surging between them just about boiled over, and she couldn't help a grin of satisfaction. Whatever lies this man might or might not be telling her, there was no lying about the urgency of his desire for her.

"A question then." She hesitated, sucking in a breath as his lips closed in on a nipple, and he nipped it lightly.

"I'm listening," he said, before his tongue curled around the nipple he'd just bitten, and sent exquisite sensations humming through her nerve endings.

Listening? she thought, somewhat dazedly. *Oh yeah. The question.* She cleared her throat. "Why not simply warn the other women to stay away from the bar?"

"It was too late," he murmured, his breath brushing coolness against the skin he'd just licked. "The killer was here days before us, and the first four victims had all decided on the men who would father a child."

Something in the way he said that made her frown. "Father a child? Isn't that putting the cart before the horse, so to speak?" After all, couples had to test the realms of compatibility in the real world before they actually discussed the option of bringing a child into the world.

"In this case, no." He lightly nipped her other breast, and she gasped, not in pain, but in pleasure.

"And that," he continued, "Was a second question."

"You said just one, but I never actually agreed to it."

His mouth moved up towards her neck, his kisses featherlight, yet burning deep. "You want me to stop?"

"God, *no.*"

His smile seemed to flow through her mind, a warmth as bright as the sun itself. "Good," he murmured, as his mouth claimed hers.

For the longest time, there was nothing but kissing and tasting and teasing. And this sort of kissing was something she'd never experienced before—because it was more than just kissing, more than just a pathway to seduction. It was as if, somewhere in the meeting of their mouths, they were becoming one in a way far deeper than even the fusing of their bodies.

Then his mouth left hers, and regret ran through her. But only for a moment, as he began to nip, lick, and kiss a blazing trail down her neck. She threw her head back and closed her eyes, enjoying his touch, enjoying the sensations that boiled through her.

And suddenly, simply enjoying his touch wasn't enough. She had to touch *him*, feel him, taste him, as thoroughly as he was tasting her.

She undid his shirt buttons and thrust the material aside, then slid her hands over his body, marveling at all the lean, hard flesh. Loving the way his skin reacted to her caress. The tremble that went through him when she plucked a nipple with two fingertips.

She kissed the base of his neck, then his pulse point, feeling a warm rush of feminine satisfaction at the way his pulse raced. No, there was no denying this man's need for her.

She raised her head and claimed his mouth once more,

kissing him fiercely but briefly.

"I need you," she whispered against his lips. "As much as you need me."

He groaned and wrapped a hand around the back of her head, pressing her forward and claiming her mouth again.

Not breaking the kiss, she rose onto her knees and reached between them, freeing him from the restrictions of his jeans. Then she thrust down on him. He groaned again, his hands sliding down to her hips, his grip bruising as he pressed her down harder. She echoed his groan and began to move. He was right there with her, kissing and touching and caressing as he moved so gloriously deep inside her. The deep down ache bloomed, becoming a kaleidoscope of sensations that washed through every corner of her mind. She thrust back her head again, gasping for breath, the air itself seeming to burn as fiercely as her skin.

Then the shuddering began and she grabbed his shoulders, pushing him deeper still, wanting to feel every inch of him through every inch of her. Pleasure began to explode as his movements become faster, more urgent.

"Look at me," he growled.

Her gaze met his, and something deep inside quivered. His eyes burned with desire and passion, but something else, something she couldn't name, seared the gray depths, stirring her in ways she didn't think possible.

"You are mine," he said, and his hoarse voice seemed to echo through her mind, through every fiber of her being.

Yes, she thought. *Yes!*

Then the passion exploded and she was quivering, trembling, whimpering, as his warmth spilled into her and his body went rigid against hers.

Finally, she collapsed against him. He wrapped his arms around her, holding her so tight it felt as if he never intended to let her go. And as much as she knew he would, she still reveled in that brief, and oh so glorious, sensation of belonging.

For several minutes neither of them moved. The air stirred around them, lifting the heat from their skin without managing to chill. From the general direction of the kitchen came the rattle of harsh breathing, and she half smiled, knowing then that Dan had indeed watched—and enjoyed. A normal woman might have been embarrassed by that knowledge, but she was a shifter. Exhibitionism was almost as natural as an extremely high sex drive.

She was just glad face shifters seemed to share the same natural urges.

Grey stirred, pushing her back from him a little before cupping her cheeks with his palms. His gaze held hers for several seconds, then he smiled, and gave her a sweet, gentle kiss. "I don't think I'm ever going to be able to get my fill of you."

Her heart did another of those uneven little dances. Did that mean he intended to keep on seeing her after the killer was caught? Lord, she hoped so.

"I thought you had a killer to catch?"

"I do. But the killer strikes at night. That gives us most of the day to play."

"I do need to get some beauty sleep, you know," she said dryly.

His thumb skimmed to her mouth, outlining it gently, sending another tremor through her. "Why? You're beautiful enough as it is."

She grinned. "You haven't seen me pre-breakfast, before coffee. Totally horrible."

"Well, technically, I have, seeing we came here to have breakfast."

"Yeah, but that's different to waking up beside me after a long night. Believe me, that can get hideous."

"Somehow, I doubt that." He slid the dress back up to her shoulders, then zipped it.

Footsteps approached as she climbed off him. She looked

over her shoulder as Grey hastily adjusted himself. It was Dan, and his smirk was as wide as the Grand Canyon. He was also carrying a pot of coffee, and she couldn't help grinning. He'd lived up to her expectations all right.

"You folks seem to be enjoying the...er...meal so much, I thought it only decent I give you a free cup of coffee."

"That's mighty nice of you," Grey said, voice bland. "But can we get that to go? We need to leave."

"That's a bit of a shame."

Her grin broke loose. "Don't think we'll make a habit of enjoying breakfast so much, Danny boy. It might not be good for your heart."

Dan met her gaze, brown eyes twinkling. "Don't you be worrying about my old ticker, lassie. And the occasional hard workout does it the world of good."

She smiled as he walked away, but the amusement quickly faded when her gaze met Grey's. "So why do we have to go?"

He nodded toward Dan. "He'll be a little more aware of what we do and say from now on. I can't answer any more questions here. It's too dangerous."

He wasn't lying, and yet...she had an odd sense that there was an ulterior motive behind his words.

"So, we find another diner. There's plenty around."

"Do you really think we can hold off touching each other in another diner?"

The look he gave her was smoldering, full of heat. And yet, she wasn't buying it. Not entirely. Oh, she had no doubt that he did want her, and want her badly, but there was also an underlying niggle that he had plans for her. Plans that she couldn't even begin to guess at.

So why did she trust him so much?

Instinct, she thought. It told her he didn't intend to harm her, and she believed that one fact totally. Whether that made her the world's biggest fool or not remained to be seen.

"I'm not sexually deprived." Well actually, she probably was, but that was beside the point. "And I think we can manage to keep our hands off each other long enough for you to answer questions."

"Your apartment would be safer. Easier."

Again with her apartment. "Why are you so determined to get me back there?"

"It's safer, simply because we don't risk being overheard." He hesitated. "In my line of work, you learn not to trust the face of the person sitting next to you."

His words had her looking over her shoulder, which was dumb when the diner was empty. "My home is my sanctuary. I rarely invite people back there."

His gaze darkened almost imperceptibly. "You still don't trust me?"

Which is not what she'd said at all, though indeed that was part of the problem. She hesitated, then said, "I have no way of checking out anything you've said, Grey. No way at all."

Anger flicked through his expression. "I thought a beagle relied on instinct?"

"They do, but I've learned to doubt."

"Then what do you suggest?" His expression had gone neutral, but there was nothing neutral about his voice as he added, "That I walk away, leave what's going on between us?"

His anger burned around her, flaying her skin as sharply as a whip. Whatever else was going on, there was no doubt in her mind that while this man might intend many things, harming her wasn't one of them. Would it be complete foolishness to let him inside her apartment? Probably. But what other choice did she really have? He seemingly had the answers she—the department—needed.

She considered him a moment longer, then said, "Give me the name of the other possible victim. I'll pass it on to my department."

"Genny Jones, Twenty-Fourth Street, Marshell apartments." He paused, then added, "It won't do them any good. They have no idea who to look for."

"Well, apparently, neither do your people; otherwise five women would not have died." She gestured toward the pay phone on the other side of the room. "Do you mind moving?"

He shifted. She climbed out of the booth and walked across to the phone. After digging her credit card out of the special compartment in her coat, she swiped it through the phone slot and dialed Jack's cell number.

He answered second ring. "Senior detective Jack Turner speaking."

"Jack? It's Eryn."

"Why the hell are you calling?" Though his voice warmed immediately, he sounded tired, almost sleepy. Maybe she'd caught him in bed. "Thought you'd be dead to the world by now."

She grinned, and refrained from reminding him she was a shifter. With a shifter's stamina. "I've got a name for you."

Bed springs squeaked, then paper rustled. "What?"

"Genny Jones. Her address is apparently the Marshell apartments, Twenty-Fourth Street."

"And she is?"

"Probably the next victim."

He paused. "I don't think I want to know how you know this."

His words suggested he'd already guessed. "We're at Greasy Dan's."

"Damn it, Eryn, you know—"

"He's not the killer."

"You willing to stake your life on that?"

Her gaze went to Grey's. He was leaning his butt against the table, his arms crossed and face absolutely expressionless. Yet she could taste his annoyance at her actions as surely as she could still smell his raw masculinity and thick desire.

"Yes." And if she let Grey into her apartment, that's exactly what she was doing—staking her life on her instincts.

"I hope you know what you're doing."

So did she. "Remember I told you about those two women at the table? I think this Genny Jones might be one of them." Which would explain why she'd smelled that aroma when she was close to them.

So how come *she* was the next one slated to die? Especially when the killer had been no where near her?

"Don't take him back to your apartment," Jack said forcefully.

"Jack, if he intended to harm me, he could have done it long before now. There's only us and Dan here in the diner. It's a perfect place for murder."

"Yeah, but your apartment is where you feel safer; therefore it's more dangerous because you're less on guard."

"I'm not a fool."

"I'm not saying you are. I'm just asking you to be careful. Especially when we know so little about this man—this *stranger*—you seem to trust so much."

"I'm being careful. I'll see you tonight."

He grunted. "You'd better."

She hung up and walked back to Grey. She stopped several feet in front of him and crossed her arms, her pose as defensive as his was hostile.

"You cannot go back to that bar tonight," he said, voice flat.

His hearing was obviously as good as hers, because she certainly hadn't been talking to Jack loudly. "I have a job to do."

"You will die doing that job."

The ice slid back into her stomach. "Why? If the killer had been anywhere near me, I would have caught his scent."

He raised his eyebrows at that. "You know his scent?"

"It lingered at the death scenes."

His expression was briefly curious. "And what did you make of it?"

She shrugged. "It almost seems more a woman's scent than a man's, except for the thick layer of death that entwines it."

Surprise flickered, not so much in his eyes, but in the air. Across her senses.

"Interesting," was all he said.

"Maybe, but you still haven't explained why I'm the next one slated to die when I've been nowhere near the killer."

He hesitated. "It will be my fault."

She raised her eyebrows. "How?"

"According to our clairvoyants, you will meet the killer tonight. He will see me in your mind, and he will snatch you, abuse you, then kill you to get at me."

"He hates you that much?"

"Yes."

"And are these killings related to his hatred of you?"

"No. I told you before what his reasons are for these killings."

She rubbed her arms, but it failed to stop the goose bumps fleeing across her skin. "And knowing all this, you still approached me last night?"

"I'd intended to walk right past you, but our gazes met." He shrugged. "I'm sorry, but I'm not superman. Even knowing the risks, I could not ignore what rose between us."

Anger surged through her. "So you endangered my life to satisfy lust?"

His anger lashed at her skin, every bit as powerful as her own. "Not lust. What lies between us is more than lust, and you know it."

"What lies between us may never have a chance to be explored any further, thanks to your behavior."

"I don't deny my stupidity, but it is a problem easily solved.

Just don't go to the bar tonight."

"I can't *not* go, especially if I'm going to meet the killer tonight."

"You will die."

"I'm in a bar, surrounded by security and watched over by police. He's not going to get me out of there without a fight. From them, and from me."

"You don't know this person. You have no idea what he's capable of."

"And despite the amazing sex we've shared, you don't know me. Nor do you know what I'm capable of."

"I don't want to see you dead."

"Believe me, it's not something I want, either."

He grimaced, then pushed away from the table and held out a hand. "We could argue about this all day. Or we could go back to your apartment, share some more of that amazing sex, and then figure out some sort of compromise that suits us both."

She glanced at her watch. It was barely eight, which still left plenty of time to play before she had to get some rest. "I really do need to sleep," she warned.

"Then I'll keep watch."

The thought of him watching her as she slept sent a thrill through her. She placed her hand in his, and he tightened his fingers, pressing warmth and an odd sense of security into her skin.

Even so, she still felt an odd reluctance to move. Not because she feared for her safety, but because she feared for something far more important—her heart. By letting Grey into her apartment, she was letting him into her sanctuary—the one place no man had ever been. It was a big step for her, and one she wasn't sure Grey would ever appreciate.

She wasn't even sure he was worthy of such a step, even if he did affect her in ways no man ever had.

But she couldn't exactly stand here, dithering, either.

"Let's go."

They were almost out the door when Dan called out, reminding them to pick up the coffee. Grey rolled his eyes, but went back to collect the cups while she huddled in the doorway. Coffee in hand and sipping it as she walked, she led him across the street and up the steps. Once there, she punched in her code, using her body to shield her movements from him. The door swung open and he ushered her through, his touch pressing warmth into her spine and sending yet another flash flood of desire crashing through her system.

Lord, even after all the sex they'd shared, it seemed her hormones couldn't get enough of this man.

They climbed the stairs to her fourth floor apartment and walked down the long corridor. Though neither of them said a word, the air grew thick and heavy, and her breathing quickened in response. And with each sharp intake of air, she breathed in his desire, his need, until it filled every corner of her body and made her burn.

Her hand trembled as she reached into her coat and took out the keycard. She swiped it through the slot, then pushed open the door and walked inside.

The door slammed shut behind her. He took the almost empty coffee container out of her hand, placing it on the hall stand, then his hands were on her, pushing her coat down her arms, pulling it off and flinging it across the room.

"I need you," he growled, kissing her shoulder, her neck, her ear. "It's madness, but I just can't seem get enough of you."

If this was madness, then she was just as insane as he. She ducked away from his kisses and spun, grabbing his shirt, popping the buttons in her haste to undress him. He threw off the shirt, then quickly shucked off his jeans. She slithered her hands down the flat of his stomach then took his cock in her fingers, relishing the way he jumped, and seemed to grow even larger under her heavy-handed caress.

He made a low noise in the back of his throat, then grasped the middle of her dress, his big hands warm on her skin. His gaze caught and held hers, his expression almost fierce. With one swift movement, he tore the material from her body and threw the remnants across the room as well.

God, she'd never been so aroused in her life.

"I need you," he repeated, then claimed her lips, his kiss harsh and urgent.

"Then take me," she said, when she could.

He did. Up against the wall, driving deep, so wonderfully deep, until it felt as if the rigid heat of him was trying to claim every inch of her. Her blood boiled through her veins, and every breath seemed a struggle, the air too thick with need and desire to breathe easily. The low down pressure began to build under the rush of passion and the sweet assault of pleasure, and all too quickly it reached the boiling point. They came as one, his roar getting lost in her howl, his body slamming into hers so hard the whole wall seemed to shake.

Then it was over, and she was trembling, sweating, her limbs so weak they seemed barely able to support her weight. She took a deep, shuddery breath, and released it slowly. "Sweet Lord, can it get any better?"

He dropped a kiss on her spine, then withdrew and turned her around. Wrapping his arms around her, he pulled her close and said, "I sure as hell want to hang around and find out."

His words made her knees want to buckle. She somehow managed to keep them locked and closed her eyes, listening to the wild beat of his heart, knowing her own raced just as badly. The smell of sweat and sex stung the air, and her nose twitched. "I think I need a shower."

Yet she couldn't move. The odd weakness was still flowing through her veins, and she was feeling more and more tired.

"I think you need sleep," he said, his breath brushing warmth against her ear.

As if his words were a trigger, she yawned. "God, I thought

it was usually the man who rolled over and went to sleep after sex."

His smile shimmered through her. "It's been a long, and strenuous, night." He pulled back, but kept one arm around her, supporting her. "Where's your bedroom?"

She waved weakly to her right. It seemed a huge effort to do even that.

"Then let's get you over there."

She nodded and walked towards her bedroom, only her feet didn't seem too inclined to follow directions, and she was stumbling more than she was walking. Only his grip kept her upright.

And through the midst of tiredness, alarm rose. This shouldn't be happening. Something was wrong.

She licked lips that suddenly seemed dry, and said, "Grey—"

"Here's your bed. You'd better lie down."

"No. There's something wrong. Something's happening to me."

He pressed her down on the bed and pulled the covers over her. "Nothing is wrong," he said, voice soothing. "You just need to sleep. To rest."

And suddenly she remembered the feeling that he had an ulterior motive for coming into her apartment. His insistence that they come here. That *he* come here.

It wasn't to love her. It was to stop her.

"How?" she murmured, the anger surging through her lost in her sleepiness and not showing in her voice.

"The coffee. I'm sorry, Eryn, but I can't let you near that place tonight." He brushed a kiss across her fingertips, then released her and stepped back. "Hate me if you will. I'd rather that than be faced with your death."

"You're damn well dead when I wake up."

He gave her a sweet half smile. "Better that than you dying. Sleep tight."

Bastard, she said again, but the words stayed locked inside. The last thing she remembered was watching him walk out the door.

Six

"Eryn!"

The voice was distant, but familiar. She murmured in annoyance, turning onto her side, wishing the sharp voice would just go away and let her sleep.

"Damn it, Eryn, wake up!"

"She can't hear you properly," a strange voice stated. "The drug is still in her system."

"Can't you give her something to counteract it?"

"I have, but it'll take a little more time."

"We haven't *got* time." Footsteps echoed, pacing from one end of her room to the other. To her sensitive ears, those steps sounded as loud as a herd of elephants.

She groaned and flung herself around, grabbing her spare pillow and dragging it over her head. Why wouldn't they just leave her be? She needed to sleep. Needed to forget.

Something stirred through her mind.

Forget?

Forget what?

Fury.

The need to chase, to bring down her quarry and get answers.

She frowned.

Chase who?

The man who'd betrayed her trust.

Grey.

Bastard.

With that word echoing through her mind, she flung the pillow off her head and sat upright.

And, at that point, realized there were men in her room. Two of them, to be precise—one of whom she didn't know.

"Thank the Lord…" The elephant steps grew closer, and

suddenly Jack appeared in her field of vision.

She blinked owlishly at him. "What the hell are you doing here?"

"What am I doing here?" he repeated, looking as frazzled as she'd ever seen him. "Don't you realize what's happened?"

She blinked again, remembering, then replied, in a voice low with anger, "Grey drugged me."

"Yeah, and it's now ten after ten. When you didn't report for work, we thought the worst."

"He didn't intend to hurt me." She reached for the glass she always kept on her bedside table, hoping the water would chase away the last cobwebs of sleep.

"We had no way of knowing that " He sat on the edge of the bed and grabbed the sheet, offering it to her. "So why did he drug you?"

She pulled the sheet up around her. She wasn't bothered by nudity and she didn't think Jack was, but she could hear other people moving about her apartment. Maybe he didn't want them finding excuses to catch a glimpse of the free breast show. "He wanted to stop me from going to the bar tonight."

"Why?"

"He said if I went there tonight, I'd die."

Jack raised an eyebrow. "Do you believe him?"

"Do I believe that he believes he's telling the truth? Yes. If you're asking if I actually believe I'd die, then no. I can't see how the killer would get me past security and all of you."

"But why does he think you'll meet the killer tonight?"

"The government mob he works for has psychics on the team. They say seven people will die before the killer is caught. They even gave him the victims' names."

"You'd think having all that information he'd be able to stop the damn killer."

She grimaced. "The killer is a face shifter. Grey has the same trouble tracking him down as we did tracking Grey."

"So why didn't they watch the victims' apartments and

vet everyone coming in or out?"

"Can you imagine the ruckus that would have caused if they'd stopped and questioned every single person coming in and out of the victims' apartment buildings? Besides, this is a *secret* government organization he works for. I don't think they'd be too happy with the sort of interest actions like that would raise."

Jack frowned. "You sure he's not just spinning you a line?"

"He's not. He gave me his full name, by the way. You can cross-check it against your search for high-society murders."

He dug an electronic notebook out of his pocket. "We came up with ten possibilities. Tell me his name and I'll cross-check now."

"Grey Harrison James McConnell—the third."

He grinned as he entered the name into the notebook. "Now that's a moniker you could hang your hat on."

"Ain't it just." She finished her glass of water and put it back on the table. "If you're here, who's running the show at the bar?"

"Bob and Henry are watching the screens. They'll give me a call if they spot anything odd."

But how would they know, given no one had any idea what their killer looked like? Except maybe Grey, and he certainly wasn't telling.

Anger rolled through her. Damn it, he was going to get it when she saw him again. She'd trusted him, and he'd drugged her. The fact that he considered it for her own good was beside the point. She'd trusted him, let him into her sanctuary, and he'd gone and done that.

Disappointing, to say the least. And a sharp reminder that no matter what might be going on between them, he was first and foremost a government man.

"What about the two women I saw at the bar last night?"

"One of them was Genny Jones, as you suspected. We've got a team staking out her apartment building. The other woman we haven't been able to trace."

She frowned. "She'd have to have credit records, wouldn't she?" And all credit cards had photo ID's on them these days.

He grimaced, though his gaze was still on the notebook. "You'd think Grey would have a credit ID somewhere, too, but apparently not."

The ice in her stomach stirred again, and her frown grew. "But that doesn't make sense."

"Nothing in this case is making a lot of sense." He paused. "Bingo. It appears your mysterious lover was telling the truth about his name."

He handed her the notebook. She quickly scanned the story, taking in the gruesome facts about the murder of his parents by rogue vampires, and the gutsy escape by him and his younger sister. Her gaze fell on the picture of the two of them. Grey was shielding his sister from the cameras, and the careful neutrality was in his eyes even then. Or maybe it was the blankness of shock. It couldn't have been easy to watch vampires tear your parents apart, then have to fight for yours and your sister's lives. Especially when you were barely ten years old.

She handed the notebook back to Jack. "What's the bar owner's name?"

A smile touched his lips. "Elizabeth Jane Magee—formally known as Elizabeth Jane McConnell."

"His sister." At least that explained Grey's certainty that the owner would not throw them out if security caught them doing the sexual tango on the dance floor.

Jack nodded. "She obviously didn't trust our ability to solve this case and called in her brother."

"Well, in some respects she was right, because we're really no closer now than we were at the beginning." They might have a scent, but a scent wasn't much good if you couldn't find the source.

"No—" A beep cut across the rest of his words. Jack stopped and pulled his cell phone from his jacket pocket. "Senior detective Jack Turner speaking."

He listened, his expression getting darker with every passing second. The ice in Eryn's stomach grew tighter. She knew, without even asking, what had happened.

She closed her eyes as he hung up, and wished she could just block her ears. She didn't want to hear what Jack was about to say. She really didn't.

"The killer has struck again," he said softly. "Genny Jones was just found dead in her apartment."

* * * *

Even with full shields up, the smell of death and blood and sheer evil was so thick in Genny Jones's apartment that Eryn had to fight the urge to spin around and walk out. She was no stranger to death, had seen it many times—and in many forms—in her years at the coroner's office, but these deaths had the power to get to her. Maybe because the killer was taking away the very things that made the victims women— and that was something *any* woman would react to.

She followed Jack into the bedroom. The forensic team was still here, so she stopped at the door, keeping her hands in her coveralls even though she wore gloves. Genny Jones's body had not yet been taken away, and like the previous victims, there was enough evidence in the rumpled state of the bed to indicate lovemaking had occurred. Eryn suspected that the samples being taken from the body would confirm this, and that the DNA would match that found on the previous victims.

Her gaze skated from the shocked expression frozen forever on Genny Jones's face, to the bloody remnants of what had once been breasts down to the gaping hole in her stomach. Though she'd seen this all before, it had been via photos. No photo on Earth could ever really convey the sickening reality. Bile rose, and she swallowed heavily.

Grey had suggested that the killer was going after these women because they had what he could not—love, acceptance. Why, then, did the killer mutilate them like this? It didn't make any sense. This was the act of someone who hated women—or at the very least, hated the things that made them women.

Jack stopped in the middle of the room and turned to face her. His expression was grim. "The scent the same?"

She nodded. "It's stronger than before. He can't have been gone all that long."

"Time of death was ten thirty-five. My people got here at ten forty." Jack's hand rose, as if to thrust his fingers through his hair before remembering that he wore the coveralls and plastic hood. "Damn it, we were watching all the entrances. None of the men Genny Jones had been seeing entered or left the building."

"Remember what he is. He could have assumed the shape of anyone living in this building. All he'd have to do was brush past him."

"Problem with that is the fact that the only men who entered were accompanied by women. Those men live here with the women that accompanied them. We've checked. They're all here, and none of them moved from their apartments."

"Then how did the killer get in without being seen? Or out?" She glanced toward the window.

"Not via them," Jack commented, obviously guessing her thoughts. "They're locked. Besides, we have cams in the building opposite."

"And you didn't see the killer?"

"Blinds were drawn in the bedroom."

"What about infrared?"

His expression, if anything, grew grimmer. "It shows them making love. It wasn't until the bedroom team made their regular check-in that anyone realized the man making love to her hadn't been seen walking into the building."

"You obviously got people over here quickly."

"But not quick enough." Jack's cell phone beeped, and he paused to answer it.

A prickle of unease skated across her skin as his expression became slightly incredulous. She crossed her arms, waiting as he told whoever was on the other end of the phone to wait where they were and he'd be right there.

"What?" she said, the minute he hung up.

He shook his head in disbelief. "One of my men has just interviewed a women four apartments down who swears a naked and bloody Genny Jones attacked her—two minutes after Genny Jones apparently died."

Eryn blinked. "Impossible."

Jack's smile was wry. "Normally, I'd think so too, but nothing in this case would surprise me any longer. Let's go talk to her."

He waved her forward, and she turned, leading the way out of the apartment, relieved to be leaving the scent of death and blood and evil. A detective stood at the door four apartments down, and he gave them access without saying a word.

Eryn paused, allowing Jack to head in first. But she'd barely crossed the threshold when the smell hit her.

The killer had been in this apartment.

She bit her lip, holding back the information as Jack questioned the old women. He got the same information his detective probably had—Genny Jones had knocked on the apartment, begging to be let in, stating that there was a man in her apartment trying to kill her. The old women had let her in and was promptly attacked and knocked unconscious. By the time she came to, there was police everywhere. Eryn rubbed her arms and met Jack's gaze. "The killer used this apartment to clean himself up."

"Probably. That doesn't explain how he escaped. Or why Genny Jones walked into this apartment a few minutes after she'd apparently died."

"No." She hesitated. "I think we need to look at the tapes." Because she had a horrible suspicion about what was going on.

And if she was right, then Grey had lied to her.

Again.

Jack studied her for a moment, then nodded and moved past her, leading the way out of the apartment and across to the truck parked discretely in a shadowed alley.

"Which tapes," he said, sliding a chair across to her while he sat in the other spare one.

"Try the entrance tapes, twenty minutes before the bedroom team report in."

Jack raised an eyebrow, but all he said was, "John?"

One of the men manning the com-screens nodded. After a few seconds, images appeared on some of the screens above them. She watched silently. About ten minutes in, she saw what she was looking for. "Freeze it," she said, and rose, pressing a finger against the screen. "Recognize her?"

Jack frowned. "Yeah. It's the woman Genny was talking to at the bar last night."

"The woman who apparently doesn't exist," she said. "Now, retrieve the tapes of the building for around the murder time, and show them on a different screen."

The young officer did. A few minutes in, she again found what she was looking for. "Freeze it," she said again, and silently pointed to the image on the screen.

"The old women," Jack said, expression incredulous. "Walking away when she was supposedly knocked out. What the hell is going on?"

"Grey told me that our killer is a freak even among the freaks. He wouldn't explain it, but I think I now know." Her gaze went back to the screen, studying the woman who was neither old nor a woman. "Our killer is a face shifter, all right, but he's something no one thought could exist—a hermaphrodite. A shifter able to take on both male and female form."

"And he's killing these women because he hates his female half," Jack said flatly.

"At a guess, yes. Why else mutilate these women the way he has?"

Jack scrubbed a hand across his face. "This doesn't exactly help us catch him."

She bit her lip, staring at the frozen image of the dark-haired woman entering the building. "Maybe it does," she said slowly. "Look at her. Doesn't she rather resemble her—his— victims? What if that's +her true form? What if she's only killing women who look like her?"

"Then we may finally have a picture to circulate. John, get us a good, close shot. And keep playing the second tape. Let's see where the old woman goes." Jack glanced at her. "If Grey was telling the truth about the number of victims, this only leaves us one—you."

She crossed her arms and began watching the tape. The fake old woman toddled up the street. "I was 'volunteered' into this to play bait. I still think that's the way to go."

"Not if you're going to end up dead."

"I have no plans to end up dead."

"I'm sure the other women would have said the same thing."

She gave him a grin. "But I have the advantage of knowing trouble might be headed my way. Besides, Grey seemed convinced that it would happen only if I went to the bar tonight."

"Grey obviously doesn't know everything, else he would have caught the killer long before now."

"True." On the screen, the old woman stepped to the curb and began waving. Soon enough, a yellow cab slid to a stop beside her.

"Get that cab's plate number, and see where he took the old woman," Jack ordered. The second of the two men in the van nodded. Jack glanced back to her. "I'm going to put a watch on your apartment. And you're going to wear tracking and audio tags at all times."

"I think that's going to extremes."

"I don't—" He stopped as his cell phone beeped again. "What is this, peak hour?" he muttered, as he reached to answer it. He was silent for a few seconds, then his silver brows rose as he glanced at her. "It's for you."

"Me?" she said, surprised. She took the phone and said, "Hello?"

"Eryn? It's Grey. Sorry to contact you via your boss, but I couldn't think of any other way to get hold of you."

Just the sound of his warm, rich voice made her heart race...and yet, there was something in his tone that made her frown. Some lack that wasn't quite right. "What's the problem?"

"We need to meet."

"Why?"

His chuckle was a low sound of desire that should have sent heat rushing across her skin. It didn't, and that only made her frown all the more.

"Why do you think?" he murmured sexily.

"Even you can't be that insatiable."

"When it comes to you, I'm afraid I am."

She bit her lip. Damn it, something was definitely off kilter, but she couldn't pinpoint exactly what.

She glanced at Jack, silently mouthing "trace the call," then said, "I'm actually not sure if I'm even speaking to you after what you did this morning."

He paused, almost for too long, then said, "I was only trying to protect you."

Her heart began to race, but with fear rather than excitement. "Knocking me out like that wasn't nice."

"But what we did beforehand was *damned* nice."

"Nothing like a sofa tango," she agreed. Jack gave her

the thumbs up, so she added, "Where would you like to meet?"

"How about your place?"

No way in hell. "How about you buy me dinner? I think you owe me that, at least."

"It's a little late, don't you think?"

"Not considering I haven't eaten all day."

He blew out a breath. "I'm afraid I don't know this city well."

He didn't? When his sister lived here? Not likely. "How about the diner where we had breakfast, then?"

He paused, and again it was overly lengthy. "Fine. How about we say in an hour?"

She glanced at her watch. It was nearly eleven-thirty. "How about we say at one? I've still got work to do."

"Fine. And don't bother to dress too fancy," he added, his husky tone sending chills rather than warmth across her skin, "because I don't plan for you to be wearing clothes for all that long."

"Can't wait," she said, and quickly disconnected.

"What was all that about?" Jack asked, shoving the phone back into his pocket.

"That was Grey, wanting to meet me."

He studied her for a moment, his expression a little confused. "You've said all along you trust him and that he's not the killer, so what's the problem?"

"I don't think it was actually Grey calling me. I think it may have been the killer."

"Why?"

"I'm not exactly sure." She hesitated. "This may sound strange, but I think it was more the lack of reaction inside me rather than anything he actually said."

Jack didn't quibble. "Then I was right—he *is* after you."

She nodded. "Where did the call come from?"

Jack glanced at the second of his men, who said, "Empty warehouse in the Yanga Park district."

She looked at Jack. "I'll bet he's holding Grey hostage in that warehouse. And I bet that's where he plans to take me after we meet at the diner."

"Again, why?"

"To kill me, of course."

He shook his head. "I mean, why hold Grey?"

"Grey said the killer hated him. He didn't say why."

"Then taking you to that warehouse to kill you is a form of torturing Grey?"

She nodded. It also meant that the killer had read Grey's mind and knew how much he cared for her.

It was a thought that sent both warmth and fear rushing through her veins. God, would fate be such a bitch as to let her glimpse possible paradise in Grey's arms, then snatch it away?

Probably.

Ignoring the chill that ran down her spine, she glanced at her watch. "If we're quick, we might be able to get to that warehouse and rescue Grey before I go to that meet."

Jack didn't move. "You sure you want to do this?"

"You want to catch the killer, don't you?"

"Yeah, but—"

"No buts," she said, with a slight smile. "You brought me onto this team to play decoy, and that's exactly what I plan to do. And it might be our one and only chance to stop this person.

Jack stared at her a moment longer, then simply said, "Let's do it."

* * * *

The wind skated around her bare legs, touching her skin with ice. Eryn shivered and rubbed her arms as she eyed the old building at the bottom of hill. Like most of the buildings around here, it had fallen into disrepair as the council and residents argued over whether this whole area should become park land or more residential space. In the meantime, it was a playground for louts, drug users, and the homeless, as well as being a nice hidey-hole for murderers.

She turned at the sound of footsteps and watched Jack approach.

"The cab let the old women off at The Commodore Hotel," he said, as he stopped.

"Hard to check the register when you have no idea what name she's using."

"True. But there was a Grey Jamison checked in. We showed the concierge Grey's pic, and it was definitely him. The front desk hasn't seen Jamison since he went up to his room early this afternoon, and he wasn't answering the phone."

Because the killer had him. Question was, how? "I gather your men checked the room?"

He nodded. "He's not there, and there was no evidence of foul play."

Meaning Grey hadn't put up a fight? Why the hell not? She rubbed her arms, her gaze drifting back to the warehouse. God, she hoped he was okay.

"Everyone's in place here," Jack continued. "Infrared reports three figures inside that warehouse."

"He left guards?"

Jack nodded. "There's one man near the front entrance, two near the back. We're guessing that if Grey *is* there, he's one of these." He handed her a Taser. "You'll have to get close for this to knock them out, but I'm guessing that with what you're almost wearing, it won't be a problem."

She slipped the Taser into the special pocket sewn into the back of the short leather skirt. Combined with the studded leather bra, the matching dog collar that now included tracking and audio mikes, and six inch stilettos that could certainly double as a weapon, she had on what she liked to describe as her eye-popping outfit. Jack had been surprised that she even *had* such an outfit in her wardrobe. He obviously thought her as staid as everyone else, but hey, she was a shifter and had her wild side—even if she didn't bring it out to play very often.

She struck a pose. "So you like what you see?"

"Darlin', if those boys don't bone up the minute they see you, I'll dye my hair pink." He handed her a riding crop and several long strips of leather. "Just to complete the look."

"I won't ask where you managed to find one of these at this hour." She looped the soft leather and tucked them into the side of her skirt, then accepted the whip. Her gaze scooted down his body. *Talk about boning up...*

She grinned. "You're enjoying your job again, I see."

"I'm a man, you're breathtaking, and a reaction is natural." His grin faded, his expression becoming serious. "Be careful in there, and remember, just give the word and we'll be with you in seconds."

She nodded, placed a kiss on his cheek, then stepped back and called to that place deep within, where the hound dog lay waiting. Energy surged in response, running through her, around her, momentarily snatching away sight and sense as it reshaped and changed her body.

In beagle form, she headed towards the warehouse.

She pricked her ears and sniffed the air as she trotted down the hill. Though she knew there were at least a dozen cops scattered around the area, she couldn't hear them, and she certainly couldn't smell them. Jack had said he'd called in the best, and it looked as if he hadn't been exaggerating.

And she knew then that the only reason she was going into that warehouse at all was because she was the only one who had a hope of sorting out friend from foe via smell. Especially if those two men in there also happened to be face shifters.

She slowed as she approached the warehouse, searching the air for the aroma of the man who stood near the entrance. Pine and musk, intermingled with the stale stench of sweat, teased her nostrils. She wrinkled her nose and moved a little closer. Damn it, why did villains never seem to bathe? Or was

it simply something in their base smell that made them seem
so sour to her senses?

She slipped in through the semi-open door and stopped
in the shadows. Villain number one was half concealed by a
wooden crate, and more than half asleep. She went back
outside, shifted shaped, then boldly thrust open the door.

There was a scramble of movement, then a voice said,
"Stop right there, and get your hands...Jesus!"

"Mr. Harding?" she said, keeping her voice low, throaty.
"I'm here, as requested."

His gaze scooted down her body, and came back up,
filled with heat. "Lady, as much as I hate to admit it, I think
you've got the wrong address."

She slapped the whip lightly against her thigh, watching
him for several long minutes. The smell of his excitement began
to stain the air. "This is one-three-four Jaybel Drive, is it not?"

"Well, yeah, but—"

"Then I have the right address." She slid her gaze slowly
down his body, then deliberately licked her lips. "I must say,
you're in better shape than some of the other clients
I've...cared for...here."

He adjusted himself quickly, cast a quick, almost furtive
look toward the shadows on his right, then looked back at
her. His change of plans was evident in the lustful light in his
eyes. "Then maybe I am Mr. Harding. What do you plan to
do for me?"

She strode towards him, her stilettos drumming a sharp
tattoo on the concrete. The noise wouldn't carry to the other
guard, simply because this warehouse was large and divided
by lots of rooms.

She stopped when there were still several feet between
them, and raised the whip, pressing the tip lightly against his
chest. "That depends on how rough you like it." She let her
gaze slide down to his hand. "That gun real, or is it a toy you
bought along for us to play with?"

He licked his lips. "What do you mean by play?"

She raised her eyebrows, and slid one hand up her thigh, pushing up the skirt and touching herself lightly. "Cold metal inserted in warm places can give a delicious thrill."

He made a strangled sort of sound, and tried to step forward. She pressed the whip harder against his chest. "Naughty boy. You paid to be spanked and dominated, not the other way around."

His breathing was becoming more and more rapid, and the scent of his desire swirled around her. Despite her utter distaste for the man, she couldn't help being a little aroused by what she was doing. Maybe this was a game she could play with someone she liked

Grey, for instance.

She smiled at the thought, and in that moment, awareness surged, a firestorm that burned through every nerve ending.

Eryn?

The voice was groggy, the question uncertain, but it was Grey, there was no doubt about that. The surge of desire and relief was evidence enough of that.

Here. She formed the answer in her mind, hoping he could read it. She'd never attempted mind communication before—hadn't even been aware she was capable of it. She slapped the whip against the guard's hip and added in a stern voice. "Strip, and do it quickly."

Strip?

Just taking care of guard number one.

By fucking him?

The question had a note of fury that made her smile.

You say that like fucking him would be a bad thing.

You are mine! The words reverberated through her mind so loudly, she couldn't help wincing. Yet they also made her heart race and her feet want to do a cheerful little dance. She was *his*.

Was it only a day ago those same words had made her

furious?

I'm only joking, Grey. I'm merely getting him naked so he thinks he's going to hit the jackpot. When I get close to him, I'll Taser him unconscious.

So what the hell are you wearing that makes him think he's going to get lucky?

Think leather, think dominatrix.

There was a long pause. *I don't think thinking about that is a good idea.*

She had to restrain her grin. *Hang on a moment. Got to take care of the guard.*

She slid the tip of the whip down the guard's chest, and lightly flicked it over his cock. He shuddered and swallowed. "Nice," she said, sliding the whip down his shaft and lightly toying with his balls. "Very nice. Turn around."

He did, his breathing so hard his whole body shook. Yet he was still a little wary—tension rode his shoulders, and he watched her over one shoulder. He still had the gun. She had to be careful.

She stepped closer, resisting the urge to wrinkle her nose at the stale smell of him. Forcing a smile, she met his gaze as she rubbed her studded bra across the width of his back. "Like that?"

His thick groan was answer enough. She snorted softly. "I'm not convinced." She stepped back and slapped the whip against his bare butt. "Spread your legs."

He did. Quickly.

"What do you want me to do, little boy?"

He gave another thick groan. "Rub your breasts up and down my back."

She gave him another slap with the whip. "I didn't hear the magic word."

"Please."

She slapped him again. "I don't believe you meant it. And who gave you permission to look at me?"

"Pretty please," he repeated, his words a shudder of excitement as he turned his head away.

She smiled grimly and reached back, wrapping her fingers around the Taser.

"Get ready," she whispered, slipping the whip between his spread legs, caressing him even as she pressed the Taser against his back. He didn't make a sound, simply collapsed. She caught the gun from his nerveless fingers, then stepped back so he could fall.

"Guard number one down and out," she said softly, more for Jack's benefit than Grey's.

She took one strip of leather from her waist and quickly hog-tied the guard. Then she shifted shape, and began weaving her way through the many rooms that separated her from Grey.

Well done, Grey said. *But I doubt the second guard will be as dense as the first.*

What can you tell me about him?

He's big. And a horse shifter.

Yum. I've never had a horse shifter before. I'm told they rather live up to a stallion's reputation.

Damn it, Eryn, enough.

His voice held that note of fury again, and she felt like laughing. If he was reacting so readily to her teasing, he did indeed care.

So, does this sudden sense of propriety mean you intend to explore our relationship further?

Not if you continue to talk about fucking other men.

I'm a mutt. Mutts have sex on the brain.

I'd rather this mutt concentrate on the business at hand—me.

I'm here because of you. And I'll do whatever it takes to get you free. But could she have sex with another man while Grey was watching? Deep down, she knew the answer was no. Grey was the only man she wanted inside her.

What else can you tell me about the guard?

His name is Leon Harvey. He's ex-military, and hired help.

So he has no loyalty to our killer?

No. And the killer's name is Marcy Jones. Though he prefers Marshall.

So he is officially a she?

Officially, yes.

Mentally?

A male who hates his feminine side.

So does he really want acceptance? Love? Or was that just a line you were spinning to get me off the track.

No line. And don't forget babies.

She frowned. *So why is he slicing these women up the way he is if he wants babies? Surely, as a male, he could find a woman to impregnate?*

His male side is sterile.

So if he wants kids, he has to rely on the very part of him he hates?

Yes. And the anger he feels is taken out on women who are similar in looks.

Which also explained how he was getting into the bars. He was going there as a fertile woman, not a sterile man.

She trotted through yet another doorway and entered a long corridor. The tang of cigarette smoke began to taint the air, along with the faint stench of burnt flesh.

Silver, she thought. They'd chained Grey with silver. Which would explain why he hadn't escaped. It would also stop her from freeing him. Silver burned, and stopped, shifters of any race. She swallowed the rising sense of sick fury and asked, *Your guard a smoker?*

Yes.

Then I must be getting close. She hesitated, sniffing the air. The scent of man was coming from the left of the doorway ahead. The scent of desire and raw masculinity from the right. *Did Ms. Marshall and Leon say anything to each other before Marshall left that would help me get close to this man?*

I was out of it a lot of the time. Grey hesitated. *He was going on about a special form of torture he had planned for me before he kills me, but that's really it.*

I think he was planning to drag me back here, torture me, then kill me, while you watched.

He phoned you, didn't he?

Said he was you.

You weren't fooled. He sounded oddly proud.

My hormones weren't fooled. She shifted shape. *I'm about to enter. Don't react.*

If you look as good as I think you do, that's going to be a little hard.

Oh, I expect you're going to be more than a little hard by the time I've finished with you.

Damn it, woman, what have you got—

You'll soon find out, she cut in, then cleared her voice and added loudly, "Leon? Leon Harvey? I'm about to enter the room, and I do not wish to be shot."

The sound of a safety being clicked off was unmistakable in the sharp silence. "Do it. With your hands up."

She raised her hands and entered the room, glancing immediately to the right.

And there she saw Grey.

Beaten and bloody.

Bruised and naked.

Tied spread-eagled to the wall behind him by silver chains that had burned deep welts into his wrists and ankles.

Fury rushed through her, but she swallowed it down and carefully schooled her face to blankness. Looking to her left, she raised an eyebrow at the man holding the gun aimed at her head and said calmly, "That the man Marshall wants me to give the full treatment to?"

Seven

The big man with black hair and bay-colored skin didn't even blink. "What are you blabbering about, woman?"

"That man." She waved a raised hand toward Grey, ensuring her skirt rode up a little bit more as she did so.

Damn, that's a mighty fine thatch your flashing there, came Grey's comment. *But I do wish you'd stop flashing it at all and sundry.*

It's my thatch, and I'll damn well flash it where I want. She hesitated, then said softly, *God, you look like shit.* To the guard, she added, "Is he the man Marshall wants treated?"

I'm far better than I look. Marcia didn't seem to want to cause me serious damage just yet. And I can see I'm going to have a lot of trouble keeping your wilder tendencies all to myself.

She hid her smile and kept her gaze on the guard. Hunger flickered in the shifter's dark eyes, but there was no other reaction. "What do you mean, treated?"

"What do you think I mean?" She allowed a saucy smile to touch her lips, and lowered her voice a notch. "There's more than one way to kill a man, you know. And some of them can be both delicious and extremely, extremely, painful."

He frowned. "I don't know anything about this."

"Then call Marshall and confirm it, because my time is expensive, and I don't think he's going to be happy if we stand here wasting it."

The big man continued to stare at her, the gun in his hand unwavering. "I think I might. I don't like the feel of this."

"Fine. Shoot me or call him. Your choice. Just do something because my arms are getting a little tired hanging here above my head." She wriggled her fingers, making the skirt rise and fall again.

He was a man. His gaze wavered briefly, and the heat in his eyes grew. Though his heat was nothing compared to the furnace running through her mind.

"I believe he should be at Dan's diner right about now," she continued, "waiting for his next...er...date. If you hurry, you should catch him before he gets down to business with her."

Marcia has a meeting with you?

I have twenty minutes to get there. Which left her five minutes to free Grey, and no time to play with this guard.

You can't meet with him.

I not only intend to meet with him, but I intend to stop him.

Not alone, you won't.

The guard frowned. "How do you know all that?"

"Maybe the fairies told me," she said dryly.

"He's paying you?"

"Big dollars for a few hours work." She arched an eyebrow, letting her gaze slide slowly down his well muscled form. "If I hurry just a little, shifter, you and I might be able to have a little fun before the boss gets back."

He lowered one weapon and raised the other. Even from where she stood, it was obvious the rumors about horse shifters were true. Man, he was *big.*

Too big for her liking.

"Is that a yes?" she added, staring pointedly at his erection.

"I can't see how you'd know what you know if you weren't on the books," he said. He pointed his chin at Grey. "What do you intend to do?"

"Oh, lots of delicious things." She lowered her arms and lightly slapped the whip against her leg. "I usually work alone, but an audience might add to the fun. You want to watch?"

I thought the idea was to get him out of the room?

The idea is to getting him so aroused by what I'm doing to you that he's not thinking straight, enabling me to get close enough to Taser him unconscious.

Hang on, say that again? What you're doing to me? What exactly are you going to do to me?

I'm not going to let this outfit go to waste, that's for sure.

His brief smile shimmered through her mind. *Remember, what you do to me, I shall do to you.*

And, oh, she couldn't wait.

She tried to calm the excitement racing through her veins and said to the guard. "Why don't you drag that box you were sitting on over to that corner there?"

She pointed the whip to the corner to the right of Grey. It put the man more in front than on the side, and would keep him from seeing the Taser tucked into the back of her skirt.

"Sounds fine to me." His voice was a little roughened by desire, and she smiled, feeling better about herself than she had in months. At the very least, the last few days had proved that, despite the sexual drought, she'd lost none of her allure as a woman.

She waited until the guard had positioned himself, then strode over to Grey.

I have never seen a sexier walk, Grey commented, smoky eyes gleaming with amusement and desire.

Hush. You're supposed to be dreading what I'm about to do.

When you're looking like that? Darling, no man would be capable of dreading what's coming.

The endearment made her heart do an odd little jig. She stopped in front of him, and pressed the whip lightly against his balls. "It seems the victim desires me."

The victim knows exactly what you're capable of, and hungers for more.

She flicked the whip upwards, lightly striking his shaft. He jumped, even though he had to know she would never hurt him.

"By the time I'm finished, this will strain and quiver to sink itself into my flesh, and you will be so mad with desire you would rip out your heart if that is what I want."

Definitely. Aloud, he said, "Lady, you kid yourself."

His voice was a harsh croak, so different from the warm richness of the voice that flowed through her mind.

She glanced at the guard, eyebrow raised. "Do you think I'm kidding?"

"I think you're capable of anything." He settled back against the wall, arms crossed and obviously ready to enjoy the show. "And I don't believe you gave him permission to speak."

"You are so right." She returned her gaze to Grey. "He needs to be punished."

"Do your damnedest," Grey said flatly, his eyes gleaming with cheeky challenge.

You'll regret that. It's just a shame I have to hurry. She ran the whip up and down his cock. "I could strike this until to you bleed, but that would lessen my fun and shorten proceedings a little too much. Perhaps, then, I should try a gentler form of punishment."

"Perhaps you should," the guard agreed eagerly. "Make him experience pleasure, then make him watch someone else achieving the pinnacle he is denied."

Now there's a self-serving suggestion if ever I've heard one. She looked back at Grey. "That's sounds like an excellent idea."

His amusement flooded her mind. As long as you promise me the pinnacle later, he said, I can endure a long foreplay.

Done deal. She dropped to her knees and took him in her mouth, moving him up and down as she turned to the guard and held his gaze. His nostrils flared, and his breathing quickened, as he undoubtedly imagined her doing the same to him. Arousal and desire stung the air, so thick every breath was filled with it.

As the salty taste of Grey's semen began to touch her taste buds, she withdrew and rose. "You," she said, pointing the whip at the guard. "Come here."

She'd never seen anyone move so fast. "Kneel," she demanded, as he drew close.

He dropped to his knees, his eyes glowing fiercely as he stared up at her expectantly.

"Do not look at me," she added, flicking the whip across his cheek.

He looked down. She reached back for the Taser, and added, "Release yourself."

His thick groan was accompanied by the sound of a zipper being pulled down.

You men are all the same, she said to Grey. *Put the little head in control, and common sense flies out the window.*

Well, in this case it's understandable. You look like every man's vision of paradise.

She couldn't help smiling. *Thanks. And I think I'll use that.*

Feel free.

So she did. "Prepare to enter paradise," she said to the guard, then reached forward, tasering him unconscious.

"Guard number two down. It's safe to come in, Jack."

She turned once again to Grey, her gaze skating across his body, taking in all the damage she really hadn't allowed herself to fully see.

She touched a hand to the deep cut across his stomach— one of many that decorated not only his stomach, but his chest, arms and legs. They'd all stopped bleeding, but the bruising underneath was just beginning to come out. Shifter or not, he'd be sore for days. "God, you really do look like shit."

Chain rattled as he tried to reach out and touch her. But the chains pulled him up short and he hissed in frustration. "Damn it, all I want to do is fold you in my arms and hold onto you, and that's the one thing I can't do right now."

"Jack, bring bolt cutters with you." She rose up on her toes and brushed a kiss across lips that looked swollen and sore. "What did she—he—do to you?"

He grimaced. "She took what I once denied her."

She touched a hand to his cheek, staring into the ethereal beauty of his eyes, seeing anger and something else, something that gave her heart wings. It was recognition of fate. Surrender to what was yet to be explored. "I don't understand."

"Nor should you, because not a lot is known about face shifters." He hesitated, taking a deep breath. "For a start, not all of us are fertile. Of the twenty that I work with, less than half the men have the ability to father children, and less than a quarter of the women. I'm fertile, as is Marcia. But the females of our race have an additional restriction—they can only get pregnant with another face shifter."

"And Marcia wanted you to father her child."

He nodded. "I told her I would not waste my seed on someone like her."

"You said that, knowing how unstable she was?"

"Yeah." He shrugged. "She wanted the truth, she got it. She's hated me ever since."

"Did she try the other fertile men?"

"Yes. And got much the same response."

"So why fixate her hate on you?"

"Because I was her first rejection, and up until that moment, I'd been pleasant to her. She probably believed I liked her."

"So this—" She indicated the chains and his spread eagle position. "Was a way of taking advantage of you? To try and force conception?"

He nodded. "She drugged me and took your form. I couldn't help reacting."

She frowned. "How did she even know about us?"

"She was at the bar when we met." He hesitated. "You remember seeing a striking blonde holding court in the corner?"

She nodded. That was where she'd forced an introduction with Harrison. No wonder she'd caught that brief scent of death—she'd been standing mere feet away from the murderer!

"That was one of her forms. She said she also wore her true form."

Which was the dark-haired woman she'd seen in the corner booth. "I saw her talking to the last victim that night, but made the connection far too late." She hesitated. "How did she catch you?"

"She came to my hotel as you."

"How? I never touched her."

"It only has to be the lightest of touches. You probably wouldn't have even noticed."

"But you knew I was drugged."

"Yeah, but I also know that the drug can effect every shifter breed differently. I thought you'd overcome the effects and had come to give me hell." He shrugged ruefully. "As you said, when a naked woman steps into the room, the little head takes control and common sense flies out the window."

The sound of footsteps began to rattle across the concrete in the other rooms. She smiled and dropped another gentle kiss on his lips. "When this is all over, remind me to kiss the rest of your bruises better."

"When this is all over, you're going to finish what you started here," he said, dropping his gaze to his fading erection.

"Gladly," she said. "But first, let's go catch that mad hermaphrodite."

* * * *

Eryn accepted the coat Jack handed her with a grunt of thanks. The night air had gone from merely bitter to freezing, and even though she already wore one coat, it just wasn't enough. Especially now that Grey's warmth no longer pressed into her back.

Her gaze roamed across the night, searching for some

sign of Grey. He'd left a few minutes ago to get into position, and had disappeared into the shadows as easily as a vampire. Obviously, there was a lot more to face shifters than anyone knew. But he'd promised to be close, promised that under no circumstances would Marcia get near enough to hurt her. She trusted that promise.

She just didn't trust Marcia.

The woman was demented, and demented minds did not think the way normal folk did.

Jack glanced at his watch. "It's time for you to get going."

She blew out a breath and nodded. The only reason Jack and his crew weren't storming the place was because everyone knew their foe might not be who they were expecting him to be. There were six people currently in the diner. Marcia could be any one of them. She might not even be wearing Grey's form—might not change until he—she—knew for certain Eryn was going to turn up. And since Marcia was a trained operative, then she'd probably see a police charge long before they got near the building.

She buttoned up the second coat and shoved her hands into the pockets. "You'll come the minute I give the word?" She knew he would, but she just wanted to hear him confirm it yet again, if only to calm the rising tide of nerves.

"Darlin', I'll come for you anytime you want me to."

She laughed, as he'd no doubt intended, and swatted him lightly on the arm. "One of these days, you're going to meet a woman ready, willing and able to take you up on your outrageous suggestions, and then you'll be in deep shit."

"Ah, but what woman is going to put up with her man getting his jollies spying on other women?" He shook his head in mock sorrow. "I love my work, and I'm not going to leave it, so love and me ain't ever going to be companions."

"Just wait. It'll happen." Her gaze went to the diner again. "Okay, I'm off."

"Just be careful."

She nodded, hunched her shoulders a little, and then stepped out into the wind. It whipped around her, blowing her hair ten different directions as she trudged towards the diner.

"Evening Eryn," Dan greeted as she blew in through the doorway. "You're a little early today, aren't you?"

She struggled to shut the door, then blew her hair out of her face as she turned around. The scent of death was evident, but the ceiling fans were slowly spinning, moving the air, moving the scent. She couldn't pinpoint where that smell was coming from.

"Or awfully late, as the case may be," she said, undoing one coat as she looked over the other patrons. None of them looked familiar. None of them smelled familiar.

As they'd suspected, Marcia had come here wearing someone else's form.

"You want a coffee?" Dan asked.

"And a burger."

She made her way past the tables, taking in the scents as she did so. None of the patrons sitting there smelled of death. Frowning, she slid into a booth next to the window, wishing there was something she could do other than simply play the helpless bait.

She crossed her arms, staring at the other customers, wondering which one of them was the fake. Marcia was here, she was sure of it, so where the hell was she? Or rather, who the hell was she?

And for that matter, where the hell was Grey? He'd promised to stay close, but there was no shiver of recognition coming from any of the people here.

So where was he, if not inside the diner?

Dan brought over her coffee and burger, and the rich smell made her stomach rumble. It was a reminder that she hadn't eaten in a long while.

"You sound pretty hungry, Missy. You want me to start

cooking another?"

"My stomach can handle one," she said with a grin. "Two before I go to bed might give me nightmares."

He nodded, and she dug into her burger, relishing it even as she kept her eyes and ears open.

Three of the patrons chattered between themselves, their topic the movie they'd just seen. Two others read newspapers, and none of them looked like villains. But then, why would they? Even if Marcia *was* one of them, she'd been at this game long enough to look "normal."

Once she'd finished the burger, she picked up her coffee and leaned back. If not for the fact that she'd caught the whiff of evil when she'd first walked in, she might have thought this a waste of time, that Marcia had decided against coming here.

But why would she do that, when she thought she had Grey at her mercy and wanted to complete her revenge against him?

It didn't make sense. So where was she? What the hell was she waiting for?

Eryn yawned hugely. God, she was so tired—which was damn surprising after she'd slept all day. But then, she thought with a grin, if you factored in her exertions with Grey, maybe it wasn't so surprising. Either way, she definitely needed stronger coffee to keep her awake. She glanced toward the kitchen and realized Dan was watching her. Had been watching her for some time.

A chill ran through her, seeming to sap her strength in an instant.

Oh God...

She glanced at the coffee cup, at the empty plate, then back at Dan. He grinned.

Only it wasn't Dan's grin. It was something colder. More deadly.

Dan wasn't Dan. Dan was Marcia.

"Jack, get in here now," she said, only the words stuck in

her throat and wouldn't come out. She thrust to her feet, the sudden movement spinning the diner around and around.

He'd put something in the food. The coffee.

She was an idiot. A complete idiot.

Dan was approaching, his footsteps seeming to reverberate through her head. There was anger in his gaze now, and something in his right hand, something he hid from the other patrons.

A knife.

A knife that flickered with blue fire under the diner's lights. It was silver.

He couldn't get her with that knife. Couldn't lodge it in her flesh. She'd never be able to shift shape if he did.

Without really thinking, she called to her hunter soul. Magic swept through her, but the drug in her veins was slowing all reactions, even the shapeshifting one. She smelled his closeness, heard the sweep of air even as her body gained beagle form. She dodged under the blade, felt the scrape of fire as it cut across the flesh along her spine, then launched herself at his throat.

He threw up his arms to protect himself. She latched onto his forearm, her teeth sinking deep into his flesh, the metallic taste of blood rushing into her mouth as she twisted and tore at his arm. He staggered backwards, his scream a sound of fury and pain combined.

Again the air screamed its warning. She released him, dropping to the ground, trying to dodge the blow. She wasn't fast enough by half. The blade sliced into her thigh, hitting bone and lodging there. Agony flared, running like wildfire through the rest of her body.

The woman hiding in Dan's friendly form laughed. It was a cold, cruel sound that abruptly cut off, then became an odd choking sound.

"I came here with orders to kill you, Marcia," Grey said, his voice as cold as Eryn had ever heard it. "It was something

I wasn't going to enjoy until now. For touching her, for lodging that knife in her flesh, I will watch you die and I will enjoy it."

"The police are coming," the man who was Marcia gasped. "You know the rules. Do nothing when discovery could occur."

Grey snorted. "The rules, in this case, stopped applying ages ago. Good-bye Marcia."

There was a slight hiss of air, another gargled sound, then the thump of a body hitting the ground. Then warm hands were on her and the knife removed.

Eryn?

His voice was warm in her mind, but it was far away, so far away.

I have to go. I can't stay and answer the questions your boss undoubtedly has. Not yet. Heat brushed across her forehead. A kiss so sweet and tender her heart ached. *It may take a while, but I'll be back. I promise you that. Just wait for me, Eryn. Please.*

Then he was gone, and all that was left was the familiar coldness of sleeping alone.

Eight

"Happy Birthday, Jack." Eryn raised her wine glass and clinked it lightly against his. "How does it feel to be over the hill and fast approaching forty?"

"Old." Amusement touched his blue eyes. "And I'm still waiting for this goddess you reckon is out there. I think I'm about ready for a woman to call my bluff and enrich my world."

She grinned. "Maybe said goddess knows you're still not ready to settle down. Maybe she's right under your nose, and you're just not looking down."

He raised an eyebrow, the amusement in his expression becoming decidedly sexy. "The woman under my nose right now is one I'd willingly party with, only she keeps refusing my offers."

"Because you're not really serious."

"Aren't I?"

"No." She took a sip of wine, then pointed with her glass at the redhead dancing with Bob. "Amy's been known to throw a lustful look or two your way."

"She's not serious, either. Trust me on that."

"You've flirted?"

"I flirt with everyone. She ran away faster than most."

Eryn grinned. "Maybe she has deep feelings she's afraid to reveal."

"I doubt it." He took a sip of wine, then said, overly casual, "So, how's your life been lately?"

She shrugged, feigning an indifference she didn't feel. "Same old same old." Back to working with boring old farts and wondering if her sex drive had upped and left.

It had been six months since she'd last seen Grey. Trust him, he'd said. Wait for him, he'd said. Well, she had, and she would, but the hope that she'd actually see him again was beginning to fade.

"You sure you don't want to come work with me?" Jack said. "We really could use your nose on a permanent basis."

"I'll think about it."

"You will?" He raised his eyebrows. "I've been nagging you for months—why the change of heart?"

"Maybe I'm tired of working with boring old farts."

"Well, I've got the paperwork all written up. Just give me the word and you're mine."

She grinned again. "Jack, I will never be yours."

His sigh was sorrowful—an effect spoiled by the cheeky gleam in his eyes. "Ain't that a sad truth. You want to dance?"

"Nope. I might go out and get some fresh air. This room is feeling a little close." Besides, she was feeling a little depressed. Or maybe even a little sorry for herself. And definitely a little angry at Grey for making promises and not keeping them.

She finished her drink in one gulp that had her head swimming, then made her way through the dancers and headed toward the backyard.

Outside, the warmth of the day still lingered, and the night was still and bright. She closed her eyes, raising her face to the silvery light of the full moon, feeling the power of it wash through her veins. Some shifters, and not all of them children, believed the full moon had the power to grant wishes. It wasn't something she believed in.

And the moon had certainly never granted any of *her* wishes.

She blew out a breath and opened her eyes. The music from the room behind her throbbed across the night, a rich sound reminding her of that first night in the bar, and the moment her gaze had met Grey's.

And once again, she experienced the sensations of that incredible moment. Her heart leapt to her throat, and her breathing stalled as the world around her seemed to fade into silence. Fierce desire surged, burning her skin, sending little beads of perspiration skittering across her flesh. And all she wanted to do was find him, press herself against him. Feel him on her, in her.

The memories were so strong, her reactions so fierce, that, for a moment, it was easy to believe that he was here, that the reactions were real rather than a response to memory.

But the night remained silent except for the music and the distant wash of sea against sand. The air was filled with the scent of the many wildflowers inhabiting Jack's untended lawn, as well as the mellow aroma of alcohol. Raw masculinity and thick desire—the only two scents she could classify as Grey's—weren't even a blip on the smell radar.

She crossed her arms, her gaze sweeping the extent of Jack's small yard. Suddenly, she felt too confined by boundaries. She needed to be alone, needed to run, needed to go...where?

The wash of water seemed to grow stronger. The sea. She needed to go see the sea. She didn't question the desire, just turned around and walked back into the house.

"Jack," she shouted, once she'd spotted him. "I'm going for a walk."

He gave her a wave of acknowledgment. She grabbed her cardigan, just in case the wind was cooler down near the water, then, after wrapping it around her shoulders, she headed out.

The streets were silent, still. No surprise, considering it was nearly three in the morning. She smiled, enjoying the peace, letting it fill her, calm her, as she strolled toward the ocean.

The wind down near the sand was every bit as cold as she'd thought it was going to be. She stopped near the steps and leaned against the railing, watching the moonlight play among the waves, wishing Grey was here to enjoy it with her.

Damn it, why couldn't she stop thinking about him tonight?

"Perhaps because I don't intend to let you stop thinking

about me," he said, his voice so close it whispered heat past her ear. "Not tonight, not ever."

Her heart did a giddy little dance, and a gasp that was all joy escaped her lips. But as she tried to turn around and face him, he stopped her, his hands so warm, yet so unbelievably gentle on her arms.

"I don't know whether to kiss you silly for coming back," she said, leaning back against him. His arms slid around her waist, holding her tight. She closed her eyes, and somehow found the strength to add, "Or smack you senseless for the heartache you've caused me."

"I'm sorry." His lips brushed her ear, sending a flash fire of desire surging through every nerve ending. "But I dared not risk seeing you again until I'd filled out the appropriate paperwork and had all the right approvals."

"You're kidding?" She leaned her head back and met his gaze. His eyes were as bright and as silver as the moon.

Perhaps the moon had listened. Perhaps she'd bought him back to her.

"Not kidding," he said, brushing his fingers down her cheek. She trembled, and his gaze darkened imperceptibly. "I told you, the mob I work for is top secret and highly classified. Anyone I intend to see on a permanent basis has to be fully checked out."

"And that took six months?"

"Bureaucracy." He shrugged.

"So I'm approved?"

"Oh, yes."

She smiled and raised a hand, hooking it around his neck. "And what about this business of seeing me permanently—don't you think I should have had a say in that before you cleared it with your people?"

"I believe," he said softly, his smile evident in his voice, "that we have already discussed the matter. You agreed to be mine."

Her knees did their usual "almost unable to support you" act. "I believe I was insane with lust at the time."

"Ah." Mischief shimmered in his eyes. "Meaning I'll have to get you mad with lust every time I want agreement on certain matters?"

"Depends on the matters in question."

"Only the important ones. The unimportant ones, like where we're going to live, I will leave to your discretion."

"Is that a proposal? To a woman who is basically a stranger?"

He grinned. "I thought we'd just agreed not to discuss important matters until you're mad with lust? Besides, I do believe you owe me a pinnacle."

Amusement bubbled through her. "Well, I suppose I do. Shall we go somewhere more private?"

"This from the woman who insists on flashing her thatch to all and sundry." He dropped a kiss on her shoulder, sending a warm shiver scampering across her skin. "Besides, moonlight is the perfect accompaniment to lovemaking, especially for shifters of every breed."

"Not when we're on the main beach road and inviting arrest." And yet, the shifter side of her did a mad caper at the thought. Exhibitionism was part of her nature. She knew it, and he knew it.

He undid the cardigan's loose knot and slid it from her shoulders, looping it carelessly around the post. "What can they see?" he said, his breath a heated caress against her skin as he kissed her ear, her neck, her rapidly beating pulse point. "A man and a woman cuddling close as they watch the ocean."

She licked her lips, closed her eyes, enjoying the sensations rioting through her.

"Of course," he continued, sliding his fingers under her top. "If the woman happens to be naked, then they might have their suspicions."

Her breath caught as he teased the hard nub of a nipple.

"If the woman is going to be naked, she insists the man be naked as well."

His throaty chuckle just about made her puddle. Lord, she was so ready for him, and he'd barely even touched her. Was there *ever* going to be a time when they could actually enjoy a *long* lovemaking session?

"What makes you think he's not naked?"

Her eyes sprang open and she looked up at him. "You're not!"

Amusement touched the lips she just wanted to kiss forever. "Aren't I?"

"You have a shirt on. I can *see* that."

"Ah, but what about the bits you can't see?"

She felt for his leg, and met bare flesh. She swallowed, as aroused by her discovery as she would have been had he touched her. "You're wearing shorts."

He shifted, and suddenly she was touching heated flesh, feeling the desire throbbing through his shaft. Felt him grow even harder under her touch.

"Oh my," was all she could think to say.

"Oh my, indeed," he agreed. "And it's been like that since you led me toward the pinnacle in that warehouse six months ago, but wouldn't let me reach it."

"Ah," she said. "Then I guess we'd better take care of unfinished matters before we move on to more leisurely discussions."

"You're not naked yet."

"And you call yourself a well trained government man? Don't they teach you basic stuff, like undressing women in a hurry?"

"The methods are rough and ready."

The deepening roughness in his voice made the low down pool of desire tremble with expectation. "I think the situation calls for such measures."

"Perhaps it does. Stand still."

He moved back a little, and she felt a little cooler without his heat radiating across her skin. Metal touched her skin, briefly cold, then her skirt and panties were falling to her feet. Where the knife had come from she didn't know, and didn't care.

"Now how am I going to go back to the party when my clothes have been sliced apart?"

His arms went around her again, and he pulled her against him. He might be wearing a shirt, but it was undone, and the warm press of flesh against flesh had her hormones dancing in delight.

"I have no intention of letting you go back to the party. I have six months of loving to catch up on. You're mine for the next week."

"I have to work."

His hands slid under her top and cupped her breasts, pressing them lightly together as his thumbs circled and teased her nipples. "You're calling in sick."

"My boss won't like that."

"I don't care what your boss likes. I only care what you like." He slid one hand back down to her stomach and pressed her back against him even harder, until it felt as if their flesh would fuse and their bodies would become one. Lord, he felt so good, so hard and hot. Heat pooled where his fingertips rested, quickly burning deep inside. "Tell me what you'd like right now, Eryn."

For a moment, the exhibitionist part of her warred with the need to simply feel him inside. The risk taker won.

She turned in his arms, and raised a hand to his cheek. "Explore me," she said softly.

"Gladly." The hunger in his eyes made her tremble deep inside. "But I'm afraid the exploration will be fast. I want you so bad it's all I can do to just stand here."

"Then perhaps the exploration should wait."

He smiled and braced his hands on either side of the railing.

"I have been waiting to taste you and touch you for six long months. Reaching the peak can damn well wait until we're *both* ready to break."

She was about to admit she'd reached that point the minute he appeared, but his mouth claimed hers. For the longest time there was nothing but this man and this kiss and the way it made her feel and the way it felt so right.

When they finally parted, both of them were breathing so heavily the wash of the ocean was barely audible. His kisses moved down her neck, reached the top of her breast. She closed her eyes, throwing her head back and arching her spine, offering him the swollen and aching peaks of her breasts. He complied with her unspoken request, running his tongue back and forth, until her whole body was shaking with the desire to feel his mouth on her nipples again. When he took in one throbbing nub and sucked on it fiercely, pleasure exploded and she groaned.

His tongue moved on, trailing liquid heat down her stomach. Anticipation sung through every fiber. When his tongue delved into her moistness, she gasped in sheer delight. His hands touched her thighs, gently pushing. She widened her stance, allowing him greater access. Sensations flowed like liquid fire through her veins, until her whole body throbbed to the tune of that gentle yet insistent touch. The quivering quickly became a tide that threatened to overload her senses.

"Oh God, stop. *Stop*," she gasped. "I want...you... inside."

He didn't hear her. Or didn't care. Just kept on tasting her with his tongue. Then the sensations did overload her, and her body bucked in elemental delight as her orgasm ripped through her. She clawed at the railing, holding on tight as she shuddered and drowned in a myriad of delicious sensations.

They'd barely begun to ease when his lips caught hers again.

"This time," he whispered against her mouth, his gaze fierce as it held hers. "You will howl your pleasure to the moon."

Then he was inside, thrusting deep, filling her, liquefying her. It felt so good, so fine, that she groaned again—a thick sound he echoed. Her body tightened against him, and the barely sated flow of pleasure began to spiral upwards again. His body plundered as his lips had plundered, and there was nothing gentle about it. The rich ache grew, spreading from that low point deep in her belly and washing quickly across the rest of her, until every inch burned and she could barely breathe.

Through it all, his gaze held hers, as if demanding she pay attention, demanding she acknowledge what lie between them. Which she had many times during the long six months that had separated them. This was little more than proof of what she'd long known.

That this was right.

They were right.

It didn't matter if they were still strangers in so many ways. They had the hours to explore each other, learn about each other. A lifetime of hours, in fact.

Marry me, Eryn. Spend your life with me. Be mine forever.

I was yours from the minute you asked me to dance, and then proceed to show me your definition of it.

His amusement bubbled through her mind, lifting her so high it felt as if they were dancing amongst the stars.

That was your fault, woman. You looked too damn hot.

That's not much of an excuse.

Who said it was an excuse?

He kissed her then, his mouth as demanding as his body. His strokes became faster, harder, so that her whole body shuddered with it and it felt as if she would shatter into a thousand pleasured pieces.

Then we've reached an agreement? came his thought.

Only if I'm not going to have to listen to you blabber through my mind every time we make love.

In other words, shut up and concentrate?

Sounds like a plan to me. She wrapped her arms around his neck and smiled into his beautiful eyes. *After all, you have a pinnacle you've waited six months to reach.*

I'm reaching it, my love.

Then take me with you.

He did.

And all she could do was thank God she'd fallen for a man who did what he was told where it mattered most.

Breinigsville, PA USA
21 July 2010
242184BV00001B/109/A